USBORNE UNDERSTANDING GEOGRAPHY
WORLD FARMING

Martyn Bramwell

Edited by
Corinne Stockley

Designed by
John Russell

Illustrated by
Andrew Beckett, Kuo Kang Chen, Chris Shields

Scientific consultants:
Dr John Wibberley and **Derek Beckerson**

Series designer:
Stephen Wright

Contributors:
Lionel Bender and **John Stidworthy**

Editorial assistant:
Fiona Watt

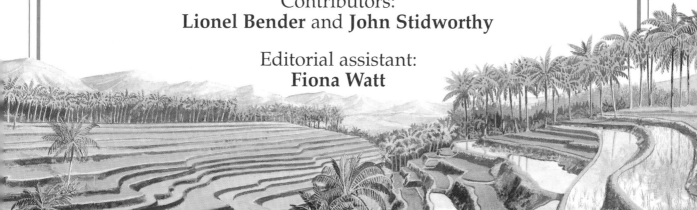

Contents

3   What is farming?
4   The first farmers
6   Climate, soil and farming
8   Food and food plants
10 Livestock
12 Grass and grazing
14 Dairy farming
16 Pig farming
18 Poultry farming
20 Mixed farming
22 Slash and burn
24 Cereal crops
26 Rice growing
28 Plantations
30 Forestry
32 Horticulture
34 Irrigation
36 Intensive farming
38 Organic farming
40 Conserving the land
42 Unusual livestock farming
44 Feeding the world
46 Glossary
48 Index

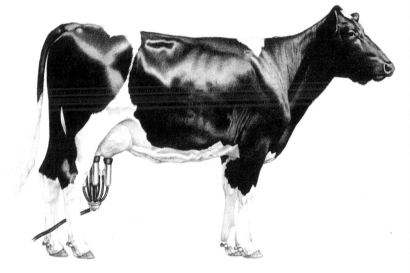

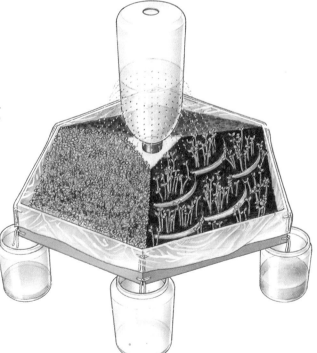

What is farming?

Farming systems are ways of organizing nature to produce food for people. There are two main types of farming - growing crops, which is called cultivation, and raising animals, which is called animal husbandry. Around the world, farming methods range from the very simple, using workers with traditional tools, to the most complex, using high-technology machines, and chemical fertilizers and pesticides. This book looks at the main kinds of farming, from the cultivation of rice paddies to vast grainlands and from raising mixed, scrubland herds to intensive poultry farming. It also examines the agricultural issues of today, such as factory farming, the over-use of chemicals, and feeding the hungry.

Activities and projects

You will find special boxes like this one in various places throughout the book. They are used for activities, experiments and projects. These will help you to understand some of the different aspects of farming. You should be able to find most of the necessary equipment at home, but you may need to go to a hardware store to buy a few of the items.

The skill in farming is to produce as much food as possible without damaging the land. This depends on the type of soil and climate, and on choosing the right crops to grow, or animals to raise. For instance, these lowland sheep would not do well on dry upland moorland, with its harsh climate and sparse, tough grass.

The first farmers

Early humans lived in wandering bands, hunting animals and gathering wild plants to eat. But between 6,000 and 10,000 years ago, in the Middle East and China, some groups began to settle in one place to raise herds of animals and grow crops to eat. These people became the first farmers.

Modern hunter-gatherers

People still live by hunting and gathering in the semi-desert and desert areas of Australia and Africa, and in the forests of Asia and South America. Their environment provides all their food, shelter, clothing, weapons and firewood.

A hunting party of Kalahari Bushmen returning to camp with a small antelope they have killed. They live on the edge of the Kalahari Desert in southwest Africa.

Farming tools

Early farmers used digging tools such as animal shoulder bones and antlers, and primitive sickles with wood or bone handles and blades made of flint. A later digging tool, the mattock, a type of heavy hoe, is still used all over the world. The first kind of plough was the ard. Ards do not roll the soil over like a modern plough does.

In many countries, fields are still prepared using traditional hand tools.

Ards are still used in many countries. The first ards were pulled by people, but later horses, oxen, camels or buffaloes were used to pull them.

An ard ploughs one furrow.

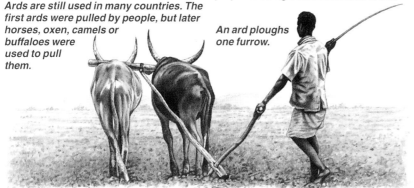

Steam-powered harvesters and other machines replaced hand tools and horse-drawn machines in the 19th century in many countries. These machines have now been replaced by powerful, complex diesel-powered machines, such as tractors and combine harvesters.

A modern tractor-drawn plough makes several furrows at the same time, and turns each slice of earth over.

Power on the farm

Until fuel-powered engines and electric motors appeared, power for such tasks as grinding corn and pumping up water was provided by wind, water, and animals such as horses, camels and oxen. Windmills and waterwheels which carry out these tasks have existed for about 2,000 years and are still in use in many countries.

An undershot waterwheel is turned by water pushing against its blades. It uses about 30% of the water's energy.

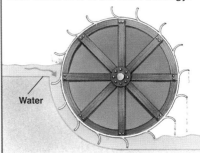

Water

An overshot waterwheel uses the pushing force of the water and also the weight of it as it falls against its blades. It is between 70% and 90% efficient.

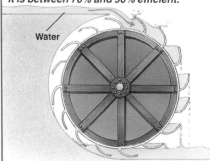

Water

There are different types of windmills. In a post windmill, the whole structure turns on a massive wooden post so that the sails face into the wind. In a cap, or bonnet, mill, just the top part is turned.

Top piece rotates

Cap mill

Capturing water's energy

This model shows how the circular motion of a waterwheel can also drive machines that need pounding and sawing movements. You may be able to think up ways of producing other movements. To make the wheel itself, you will need a clean, empty family-size ice cream tub (4 litres or 1 gallon), two round plastic lids (for example, from empty margarine tubs), a cotton reel, a knitting needle, a craft knife, two pieces of polystyrene and 12 flat pieces of plastic, each measuring 5cm x 5cm (2in x 2in), cut from any type of plastic food tub.

1. Make a hole for the knitting needle through the middle of each lid. Place the cotton reel centrally over the hole and draw around it. Using a craft knife, make twelve 5cm (2in) cuts from the circle outward.

2. Make holes (slightly bigger than in the lids) in opposite sides of the ice-cream tub and assemble the wheel as shown.

To attach some mechanical devices, you will need a cork cut in two, a plastic drinking straw, a toilet roll tube, some pins and glue, a large piece of stiff cardboard and some pieces of thick and thin cardboard.

1. Glue the large piece of cardboard to the side of the tub (make a hole to let the knitting needle through).

2. Cut a 2cm (¾in) section from the toilet roll tube, make two creases 2cm (¾in) apart and bend it to make the shape which forms a cam. Cut out two thin cardboard pieces for the open ends and glue them on. Make a hole in one cork piece, glue it to the cam and, when dry, push the whole unit, cork first, onto the needle.

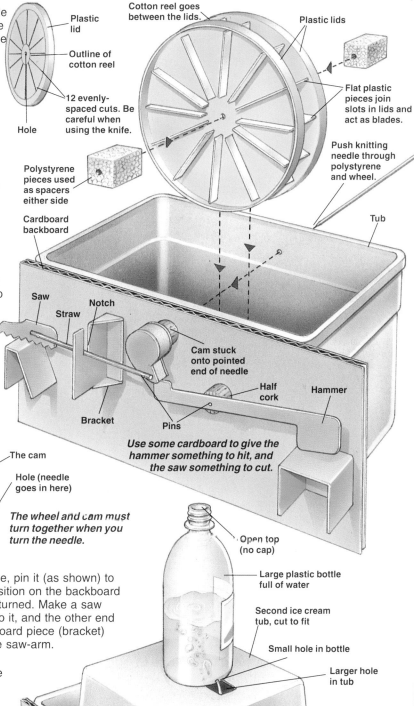

Plastic lid • **Outline of cotton reel** • **12 evenly-spaced cuts. Be careful when using the knife.** • **Hole**

Cotton reel goes between the lids.

Plastic lids

Flat plastic pieces join slots in lids and act as blades.

Push knitting needle through polystyrene and wheel.

Polystyrene pieces used as spacers either side

Cardboard backboard

Tub

Saw • Notch • Straw • Cam stuck onto pointed end of needle • Half cork • Hammer • Bracket • Pins

Use some cardboard to give the hammer something to hit, and the saw something to cut.

Piece of tube • Creases • Stick cardboard shapes on either side. • Half cork

The cam • Hole (needle goes in here)

The wheel and cam must turn together when you turn the needle.

Open top (no cap)

Large plastic bottle full of water

Second ice cream tub, cut to fit

Small hole in bottle

Larger hole in tub

3. Cut out a cardboard hammer shape, pin it (as shown) to the other cork piece and glue it in position on the backboard so it lifts and drops when the cam is turned. Make a saw shape and pin one end of the straw to it, and the other end to the point of the cam. Glue a cardboard piece (bracket) to the backboard, with a notch for the saw-arm.

4. The wheel will turn and operate the devices when you pour water on it from above, but you could set up a "waterfall" system as shown.

Climate, soil and farming

Without the right conditions of climate and soil, no plants would grow and there would be no animal life on Earth. Different types of wild plants, and farmed crops, grow best in different areas, depending on the amounts of sun and rain, and the types of soil. The map below shows the different basic climate types of the world. The most fertile areas for farming are in the temperate regions.

Tropical rainy climates - hot and wet all year. Soils are yellow or red and not very fertile, as the rain washes out their goodness. Rice and cassava are grown, but the main crops, rubber, oil and cocoa, come from forest plants and are now cultivated for export.

Warm, dry climates. The dry grassland and semi-desert areas have rocky or sandy soils which are difficult to farm, but some of the soils can be quite fertile if they are artificially watered. Crops include some grains, fruits and vegetables.

Temperate climates - mild and damp. Richest farmland areas, producing a huge variety of crops, e.g. cereals, roots, green vegetables, fruits, cotton and pasture for dairy cattle. Fertile soils, rich in minerals, include dark prairie soil and brown deciduous woodland soil.

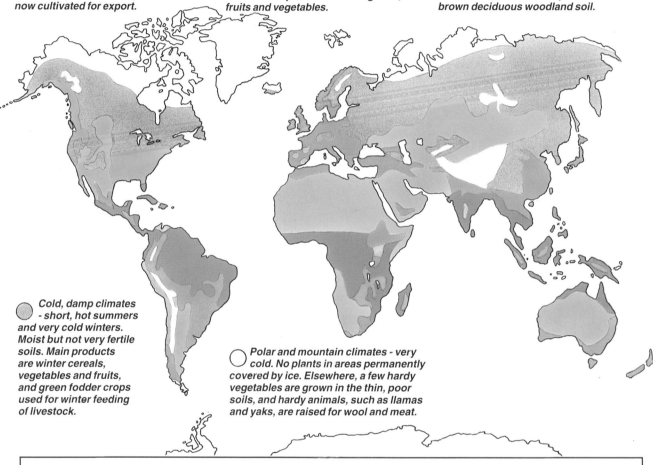

Cold, damp climates - short, hot summers and very cold winters. Moist but not very fertile soils. Main products are winter cereals, vegetables and fruits, and green fodder crops used for winter feeding of livestock.

Polar and mountain climates - very cold. No plants in areas permanently covered by ice. Elsewhere, a few hardy vegetables are grown in the thin, poor soils, and hardy animals, such as llamas and yaks, are raised for wool and meat.

What is soil?

Soil consists mainly of tiny, broken down rock particles called mineral matter, which are produced as surface rocks are worn away by the wind and rain. It also contains organic matter - the rotting remains of dead plants and animals, and animal "cast-offs" such as hair and droppings. When this has almost completely rotted, it is called humus. Humus is very important, as it binds the soil particles together and holds in moisture. It also provides many of the nutrients, (chemicals such as nitrates) that plants need to take in.

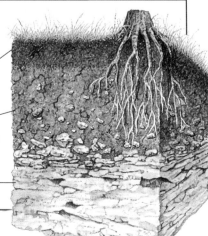

A typical farm soil has three main layers.

Cultivated topsoil, rich in humus, nutrients, earthworms and other tiny creatures

Subsoil - more mineral matter than humus. In good soil, cracks help rainwater and roots to reach deep down.

Solid rock, broken into pieces near the top and only reached by the deepest roots

The hidden workers

A very important ingredient of soil is its living population. Millions of organisms, from microscopic bacteria and fungi to worms and burrowing beetles, help break down the plant and animal remains, releasing the vital chemical nutrients back into the soil where they can be used again. The soil-dwellers also mix the soil, letting in air and helping drainage.

Without this natural recycling system, the Earth would be covered in a layer of dead plants and animals, and there would be no nutrient supply to feed new plant growth.

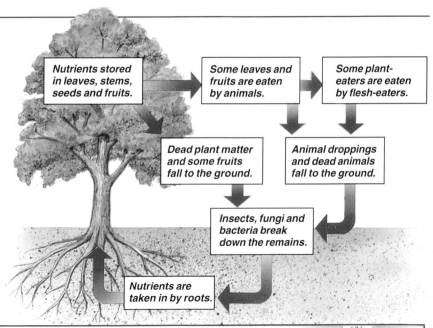

Nutrients stored in leaves, stems, seeds and fruits.

Some leaves and fruits are eaten by animals.

Some plant-eaters are eaten by flesh-eaters.

Dead plant matter and some fruits fall to the ground.

Animal droppings and dead animals fall to the ground.

Insects, fungi and bacteria break down the remains.

Nutrients are taken in by roots.

What lives in the soil?

This project will give you some idea of the range of tiny animals that live in your soil. You will need a coarse (loosely-meshed) sieve, a piece of fine mesh (taken from an old, tightly-meshed sieve) or a piece of fine gauze or muslin, a food can (or other container) with its ends removed, a plastic funnel (or a home-made one, made from stiff paper or thin cardboard), a wide-necked glass jar, a desk lamp with a 25W bulb, a small dish or tray, a small paintbrush and a magnifying glass.

1. Fix the piece of fine mesh or gauze over one end of the can using adhesive tape or glue. Place the funnel into the neck of the jar, then stand the can in the funnel.

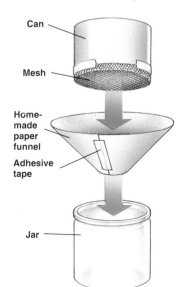

Can

Mesh

Home-made paper funnel

Adhesive tape

Jar

2. Put a sample of soil through the coarse sieve to remove any sticks, stones and earthworms, then place the soil in the can, position the lamp so that it shines down from above and switch it on. The heat from the bulb will warm up the soil.

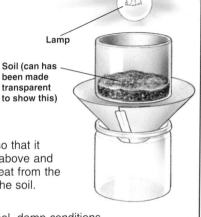

Lamp

Soil (can has been made transparent to show this)

Soil animals like cool, damp conditions, so they move away from the heat and drop through the mesh. After a few hours, tip the jar's contents, which will just look like dust and dirt, onto a dish. Use the brush to help sort out the animals and examine them closely with your magnifier.

Common animals you might find in soil. Use a field guide to help you identify others.

False scorpion

Pill millipede

Springtail

Mite

Nematode worm

A fragile resource

If soil is looked after properly, it can be used again and again, but if it is treated badly, many problems can be caused. Soils in mountain and semi-desert areas are most at risk. If too many trees, shrubs and grasses are removed by people or by grazing animals, the soil becomes low in binding humus, and is soon washed away by rain, or blown away by the wind. This process is called soil erosion and causes desertification. Areas which are affected by desertification become like deserts, with bare rock or sand covering the surface.

Too many grazing goats and cattle is one of the reasons why the Sahara Desert in Senegal grows southward by more than 100m (330ft) a year.

Food and food plants

All animals, including people, depend on plants for their food. They either eat plants, or they eat other animals that eat plants. Unlike animals, plants can make their own food. This is a simple kind of sugar called glucose and it is made by using sunlight in a process called photosynthesis. Plants also take in a number of chemicals, such as nitrates and various minerals, from the soil. These chemicals are vital to all the living things which eat them.

Photosynthesis

During photosynthesis, which means "building with light", a plant takes in water and carbon dioxide, and turns them into carbon, hydrogen and oxygen atoms. The atoms are then reassembled as glucose, and spare oxygen is given off. The Sun's energy is used to drive the process. Photosynthesis happens in the green parts of a plant, mainly the leaves, and would not be possible without the presence of a chemical called chlorophyll.

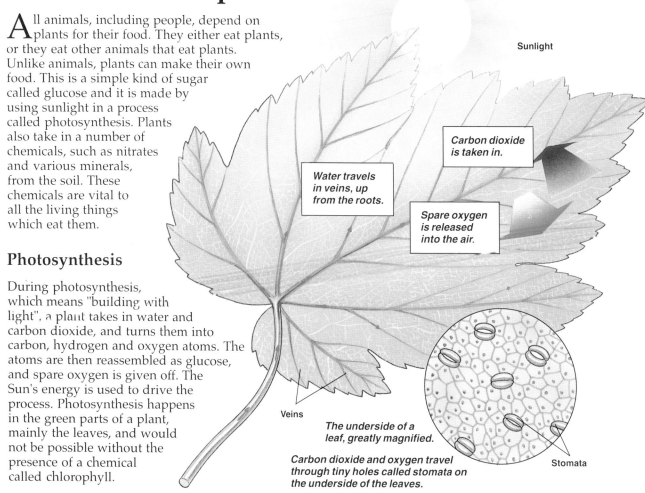

Sunlight

Carbon dioxide is taken in.

Water travels in veins, up from the roots.

Spare oxygen is released into the air.

Veins

The underside of a leaf, greatly magnified.

Stomata

Carbon dioxide and oxygen travel through tiny holes called stomata on the underside of the leaves.

Using the food

Both plants and animals need the glucose that plants make. Some of it is "burned" as fuel inside them, giving them the energy to live and grow. The rest of the glucose is changed into other substances which either become new growth material, such as new plant leaves or animal muscles, or are stored for later use. In plants, the main growth material is cellulose, a tough material used to build new cell walls, and the storage substance is starch. Starch grains are found in the stems, leaves, and especially the parts that will produce new plants.

We eat many parts of plants for their starch, but we cannot digest the cellulose. It passes through us as "fibre", which helps move other food along. Some animals, such as sheep and goats, can digest cellulose. They can eat tough leaves, twigs and even tree bark.

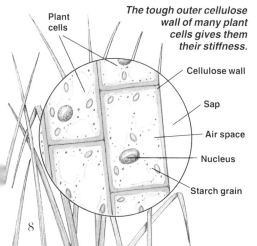

Plant cells

The tough outer cellulose wall of many plant cells gives them their stiffness.

Cellulose wall

Sap

Air space

Nucleus

Starch grain

Stores for new plants

Most plants produce seeds, from which new plants grow. Each seed contains a root, a shoot and tiny leaves packed with starch to feed the new plant as it starts to grow. Some plants also grow special, starch-filled underground roots, bulbs or stems. These stay alive while the stems and leaves die, and use the starch for energy to send up shoots when conditions are right.

Potatoes are starch-filled underground stems. If they are kept in a cool, dark place, they will start new plants by sending out shoots.

Shoot

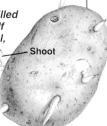

Using nature's stores

Growing crops for harvesting is called cultivation. Farmers grow many kinds of plants to harvest the parts where starch is stored, especially the seeds, roots and stems. These are the parts which are mainly eaten. As well as glucose, which we get from breaking down the starch, some of these parts also provide us with important minerals and vitamins.

A selection of plant crops

Potatoes and sweet potatoes (underground stems)

Pulses (seeds), e.g. peas and beans

Cereal grains (seeds), e.g. wheat, barley and rice

Carrots (roots)

Sugar beet (roots)

Cabbage leaves

Rhubarb (stems)

Asparagus (young shoots)

Fruits are also grown and harvested. They are mainly water, but some do contain useful substances, for example, vitamin C.

Creating better crops

Many characteristics of crops, such as size and taste, have been improved by selective breeding. Seeds for the next crop are taken from the plants which produce the best results, for instance the ones with the best-tasting fruit.

Modern wheat was developed from wild wheat by selective breeding.

Wild wheat has tiny seeds that drop off as soon as they ripen and are scattered by the wind.

The bigger seeds of modern wheat stay on the plant, so there is less waste at harvest time.

Getting started

If conditions are right for a seed, in terms of warmth, moisture and light, it will germinate (begin to grow). It takes in water through a tiny hole, called the micropyle, and swells up. Its tough seedcase splits, and the root and shoot emerge. To watch some different seeds germinate, you will need three jam jars, three sheets of blotting paper and some seeds, for example broad beans, French beans and maize.

1. Roll up a sheet of the blotting paper and place it in one of the jars, so that it springs out against the sides. Dribble water in and tilt the jar until the paper is damp.

Move the water around until all the paper is damp.

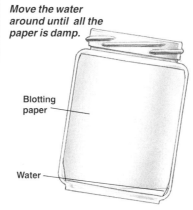

Blotting paper

Water

2. Carefully push several broad beans down between the paper and the inside of the glass.

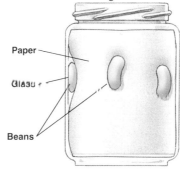

Paper

Glass

Beans

3. Do the same with the other jars using the French beans and the maize. Leave the jars by a window for 10-14 days, keeping the paper damp. The seeds will send out roots and shoots, but in different ways.

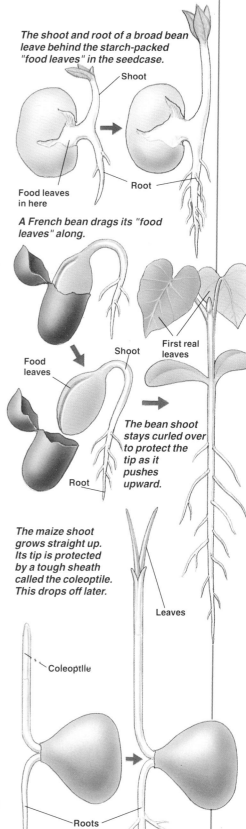

The shoot and root of a broad bean leave behind the starch-packed "food leaves" in the seedcase.

Shoot

Food leaves in here

Root

A French bean drags its "food leaves" along.

Food leaves

Shoot

First real leaves

The bean shoot stays curled over to protect the tip as it pushes upward.

Root

The maize shoot grows straight up. Its tip is protected by a tough sheath called the coleoptile. This drops off later.

Leaves

Coleoptile

Roots

Livestock

For thousands of years animals have been raised for meat, milk and eggs, which are all important sources of protein, as well as for other products such as hides (animal skins). Animals that are kept for produce are known as livestock and keeping animals is called animal husbandry. Many farmers specialize in this, while others have mixed farms where they grow crops as well as raising animals. The way farmers raise their animals depends primarily on their land, but also the kind of produce, such as meat, milk or wool, they wish to sell. They then choose the type, or breed, of animal which is most suitable.

These animals are a few examples of different breeds, kept for their products.

Animal products and uses

Beef cattle are kept for their meat, dairy cattle are kept for their milk and a few breeds are kept for both. Their hides may be made into leather and their dung used as fertilizer. In parts of Europe and Asia, cattle pull ploughs and carts, and their dung is used as fuel. Sheep and goats provide meat, milk, hides and wool. In South America, alpacas are kept for wool and llamas are kept as pack animals.

CATTLE

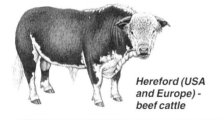

Hereford (USA and Europe) - beef cattle

Texas longhorn (USA) - beef cattle

Kankrej (India) - dairy and work animal

Friesian (Northern Europe) - dairy cattle

SHEEP

Dalesbred (UK) - kept for wool

Merino (Spain) - kept for wool

Mongolian (Central and Eastern Europe) - kept for wool and milk

GOATS

Saanen (Europe) - kept for milk

Angora (Asia) - kept for meat, hides and wool

Spin your own yarn

If you can find or buy any raw sheep's wool, for example from fields or fences, or from a farmer at shearing time, you can try spinning your own yarn. First, you should wash and disinfect the wool thoroughly. Then, you need a lid from a jam jar with a hole in the middle, some playdough, about 40cm (15½in) of knitting yarn, and a wooden stick, pointed at one end and about 40cm (15½in) long (you could use a large knitting needle).

1. Push the stick about 5cm (2in) through the hole and secure it under the lid with playdough. Tie the knitting yarn around the stick above the lid and pass it under the lid, around the stick and up again. Then make a half-hitch (over-under loop) around the stick about two-thirds of the way up.

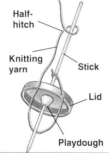

Half-hitch

Knitting yarn

Stick

Lid

Playdough

2. Twist a thick strand of raw wool onto the end of the knitting yarn (tie them together if they keep coming loose). Hold the wool in one hand. Spin the stick with the other, and let it go, so that it spins on its own. Let it spin on the floor, and hold the wool above it, using your free hand to pull out more raw wool.

3. The stick will not spin for long, so you must keep setting it off again. When you have spun a short length of new yarn, undo the half-hitch and wind the knitting yarn and new, spun yarn around the stick above the lid. Leave about 40cm (15½in) of the yarn free, make a new half-hitch and then start again.

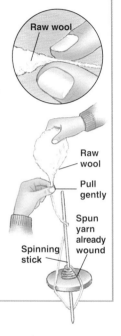

Raw wool

Raw wool

Pull gently

Spun yarn already wound

Spinning stick

Animal breeding

Each different type of animal is called a breed, but breeding itself means producing new young animals. A livestock farmer must make sure his animals breed successfully. Males and females are brought together to mate - the male puts his sperm inside the female to fertilize her (make her pregnant). On small farms, nearby farmers' animals may be mated together, but specialized livestock farms may use artificial methods (see right).

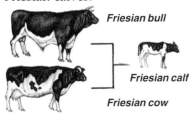

Female pig (sow)   Male pig (boar)

Selective breeding

As with crops, "better" animals can be produced by selective breeding. The best males and females are mated with each other so they produce the best offspring. The "best" could be, for instance, the fastest growing. Mating two animals of the same breed is called pure breeding. For example, mating the best Friesian bull and cow will produce top-quality Friesian calves.

Friesian bull

Friesian calf

Friesian cow

Crossbreeding is the mating of two animals of different breeds. Each new animal born is of a new, mixed breed and is called a hybrid or a cross. This term also used for any plant which has been cross-bred. It has some of the qualities of each parent and may even have a little bit extra. It may, for instance, give more milk than either of the parent breeds or grow faster. This is called hybrid vigour.

Artificial insemination (AI)

Artificial insemination allows farmers to produce new animals without bringing males and females together to mate. It is used mainly with cattle. The farmers buy bulls' semen (the liquid containing their sperm) from a farm which has bulls and the special equipment needed to collect the semen. They place the semen inside their cows. AI allows farmers to breed top-quality animals without the huge cost of owning a prize bull.

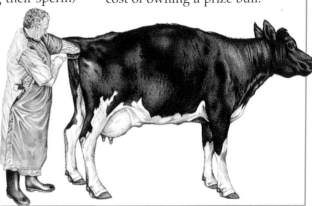

The farm selling the semen may be far away, so the semen is deep-frozen for its journey.

The semen is placed inside the cows using a long tube. The farmer puts his arm up inside the cow to guide the tube into position.

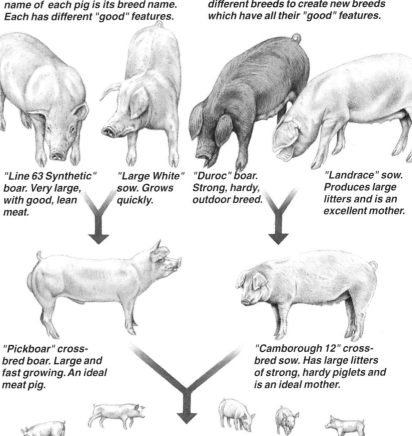

A crossbreeding "family tree" - the name of each pig is its breed name. Each has different "good" features.

The breeder mates together pigs of different breeds to create new breeds which have all their "good" features.

"Line 63 Synthetic" boar. Very large, with good, lean meat.

"Large White" sow. Grows quickly.

"Duroc" boar. Strong, hardy, outdoor breed.

"Landrace" sow. Produces large litters and is an excellent mother.

"Pickboar" cross-bred boar. Large and fast growing. An ideal meat pig.

"Camborough 12" cross-bred sow. Has large litters of strong, hardy piglets and is an ideal mother.

The piglets are fast-growing, lean, strong and healthy, combining all the "good" features.

Grass and grazing

Grasslands cover almost a quarter of the world's land and provide grazing land for about 1,200 million cattle, 1,300 million sheep and 450 million goats. These animals, together with others such as yaks and deer, can feed on grass and leaves because, unlike us, they can digest cellulose. Their complex stomachs contain bacteria which break up the cellulose. The process is helped by the animals bringing food back up into their mouths to chew it again. This is known as chewing the cud.

Animal management

The quality of grazing land varies greatly around the world, from sparse, tough grasses to rich, fertile pasture. To a large extent, this dictates the way that animals are reared and managed. On poor land with little food, for example, the animals are spread out over vast areas, often known as ranches, and are rounded up only for dipping, shearing or to be taken to market. This system is called extensive farming and is widespread in Australia, New Zealand, Argentina, Brazil and the southern and midwestern states of the US.

When sheep are dipped they are completely submerged in a large trough of insecticide. This kills fly larvae and other parasites on their skin. In many countries regular dipping is required by law.

On better-quality land, the animals need not be so spread out. They are often fenced in so that one area is grazed at a time. The farmer can enrich the pasture with fertilizers, such as chemicals or animal manure, keep a closer watch on the health of the animals and improve the herd by careful breeding.

Small herds and herders

Not all livestock herders have large herds. In many areas of the world, relatively small herds are kept. Some herders may keep just a few cattle, sheep or goats. Many of these herders live in desert, semi-desert, mountain and Arctic areas and, like the ranchers in an extensive farming system, they have the problem of poor land, with sparse vegetation, so there is little food for their animals.

The Sami (Lapps) of Scandinavia keep herds of reindeer to provide meat, milk and hides, and to carry goods and pull sledges over the snow.

On South American cattle ranches, the herds are patrolled and rounded up by horse riders called gauchos (South American cowboys).

The animals range over vast areas of poor quality grass.

Some herders lead a nomadic or wandering life, allowing their small herds to roam free. They follow their animals on their migrations from summer to winter feeding areas and back.

A mixed flock of sheep and goats in North Africa. The sheep eat grass while the goats nibble the leaves of bushes. They do not compete for food, so both can survive on the poor vegetation.

Animals which chew the cud, such as cattle, are called ruminants.

Intensive livestock farming

If they can afford expensive farm chemicals and high-technology machines, and if the demand for their produce makes this expense worthwhile, many livestock farmers use intensive farming methods to increase their meat or milk production. Intensive livestock farming means that animals graze on pastures enriched with fertilizers, and are also given concentrated food to help them grow quickly. They are normally brought inside in the winter and fed on fodder crops and silage, made from cut grass, though in some intensive systems the animals are kept indoors for the whole year.

The beef feedlot system is an intensive livestock system. The cattle are kept in enclosures all year long, and are fed on fodder crops, as well as food concentrates and silage.

Pests and diseases

Cattle, sheep and goats can suffer from many different diseases, which livestock farmers must fight. For instance, cattle are affected by diseases such as mastitis, brucellosis and foot-and-mouth disease, any of which can be fatal. West African cattle are particularly affected by a fatal disease, called trypanosomiasis, caused by a tiny parasite, passed between animals by the tsetse fly as it feeds on their blood. Sheep that eat damp grass can get liver rot if they take in tiny bodies called cysts, which develop into liver flukes inside them.

Life cycle of liver fluke

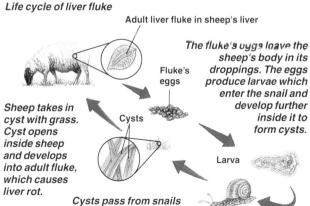

Adult liver fluke in sheep's liver

Fluke's eggs

The fluke's eggs leave the sheep's body in its droppings. The eggs produce larvae which enter the snail and develop further inside it to form cysts.

Sheep takes in cyst with grass. Cyst opens inside sheep and develops into adult fluke, which causes liver rot.

Cysts

Larva

Cysts pass from snails onto grassland.

Dairy farming

In many parts of the world, milk and other dairy products, such as cheese and yogurt, are very important in human nutrition. Most people use cow's milk although some use milk from goats, sheep, camels, reindeer, yaks or buffaloes.

Dairy herds

In the developed world, large herds of cows are raised just for milk, on dairy farms. The cows need richer, better quality pasture and more drinking water than beef cattle in order to turn as much of their food as possible into milk, rather than muscle (meat). Popular breeds include Friesians, Jerseys and Holsteins.

A typical dairy cow produces approximately 5000 litres (1500 US gallons) of milk a year. The world's top milkers may give up to 16,000 litres (4000 US gallons).

Friesian cow

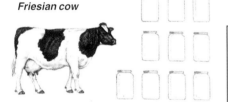

In the developing world, herds are usually small because of poor pasture. They are often a mixture of sheep, goats and cattle, and animals kept for their meat and other products as well as milk. The most common breeds are members of the Zebu family, with their characteristic hump and drooping ears. Unlike most of the non-tropical breeds, they can survive the hot climate and the cattle diseases of the tropics.

Milk production is low in the developing world, often as little as 50 litres (13 US gallons) in a year.

Nellore (Zebu breed)

The dairy cow cycle

A cow produces milk to feed her calf, so before a dairy cow can start producing milk, she must have a calf. Most cows on dairy farms in the developed world have their first calf at two years old, and have five or six during their working life. Some farmers mate their cows so they calve in the spring when food is plentiful, others go for autumn calving because they get a higher price for their milk in the winter months.

On the right is the milk production cycle for a cow with autumn calvings. It begins in early September. The strength of colour of the inner ring shows the quality of milk produced.

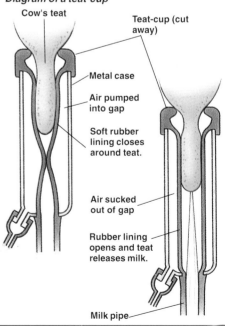

DEC

NOV

Cow mated again

Peak yield

OCT

SEP

Colostrum stage

Calf born (autumn calving)

Milking

On a modern dairy farm, all the milking is done by machine. Mechanized teat-cups suck the milk from the cow's udders, and it is piped to collecting jars, or through flow-meters, to measure the quantity. It then goes into a refrigerated storage tank before being taken, by tankers, to the bottling plant for processing.

A herringbone milking shed. The cows stand at an angle to the central pit.

Teat-cup cluster

The central pit is for herdsmen, who clean the udders and attach the teat-cups.

Teat-cups imitate a calf's sucking action. A pulsator unit rhythmically alters the air pressure inside them.

Diagram of a teat-cup

Cow's teat

Teat-cup (cut away)

Metal case

Air pumped into gap

Soft rubber lining closes around teat.

Air sucked out of gap

Rubber lining opens and teat releases milk.

Milk pipe

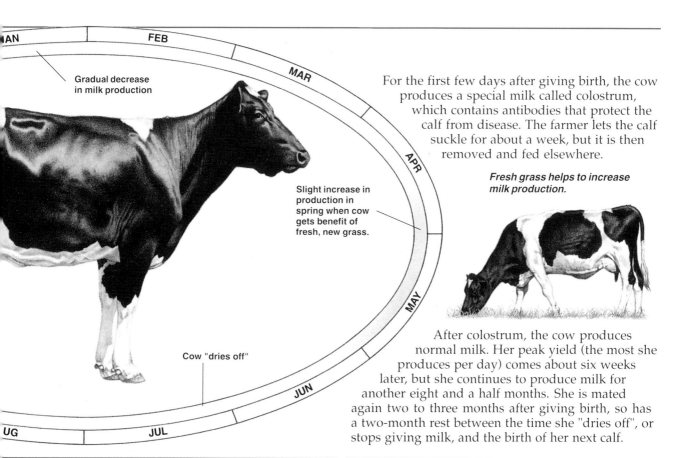

JAN   FEB   MAR   APR   MAY   JUN   JUL   AUG

Gradual decrease in milk production

Slight increase in production in spring when cow gets benefit of fresh, new grass.

Cow "dries off"

For the first few days after giving birth, the cow produces a special milk called colostrum, which contains antibodies that protect the calf from disease. The farmer lets the calf suckle for about a week, but it is then removed and fed elsewhere.

Fresh grass helps to increase milk production.

After colostrum, the cow produces normal milk. Her peak yield (the most she produces per day) comes about six weeks later, but she continues to produce milk for another eight and a half months. She is mated again two to three months after giving birth, so has a two-month rest between the time she "dries off", or stops giving milk, and the birth of her next calf.

In the developing world, most milking is still done by hand. The teat is squeezed between the thumb and forefinger and the hand is pulled firmly, but gently, downward, squeezing out the milk.

Hand milking

Teat grasped gently and pushed up slightly.

Teat is squeezed and pulled down, causing the milk to flow downward.

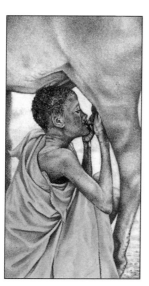

A woman in East Africa drinking straight from a teat.

Make your own yogurt

Yogurt is a semi-solid food made from milk that has been altered by special kinds of bacteria. To make some home-made yogurt, you will need 575ml (2½ US cups) of fresh milk, 50g (½ US cup) of dried skimmed milk, 1 tablespoon of plain natural (live) yogurt, a vacuum flask and a cookery thermometer.

1. Heat the milk to 48°C (109°F) and stir in the skimmed milk and yogurt.

2 Fill a vacuum flask with hot water to warm it up. Then pour out the water, pour in the milk mixture and seal the flask. Leave it for several hours for the bacteria to act.

3. Place the flask in the refrigerator, and leave it for four hours. Then add sweetener or fruit to the yogurt and eat within five days. Store it in a refrigerator at all times.

Pig farming

About 800 million pigs are kept around the world. Over half of them are in Asia, where pork is the main meat eaten. Farm pigs are descended from wild pigs which people began to domesticate almost 9,000 years ago. This may have happened because pigs eat many of the same things as people and the wild pigs may have scavenged for food around their settlements. Modern pig farmers use either outdoor or indoor systems.

Wild relatives of the domestic pig include the African warthog and the strange, four-tusked Indonesian babirusa.

Farm pigs are descended from wild boars which still live in forests in many countries. A farm pig may weigh twice as much as a wild boar, however.

Indonesian babirusa

Wild boar, or Eurasian wild pig

African warthog

Raising piglets

Young female pigs are called gilts. They are first mated with males (boars) at seven months old. It takes about 16 weeks from mating to the birth of the litter of piglets. Once they have given birth, the females are called sows. The piglets suckle for about three to six weeks and are then weaned (taken off their mother's milk). The sows are ready to mate again after another week.

Piglets' sharp eye teeth are removed, their tails are docked and they receive injections of iron and antibiotics.

Feeding and watering

Once weaned, most pigs are fed on concentrated pig meal made of cereals, fish meal, bone meal, skimmed milk and vitamins, though traditionally in parts of Europe they are fattened up on acorns in oak forests or fallen fruit in orchards. They grow very quickly and are among the most efficient farm animals at turning food into meat. They weigh about 1kg (2¼lb) at birth, and are fattened in six to eight months, to 70kg (154lb) to be killed for pork, to 90kg (198lb) for bacon and to 100kg (220lb) for sausage meat. As with all animals raised for meat, some are kept alive to breed from.

As well as lots of food, each pig also needs up to 9 litres (2⅓ US gallons) of water per day.

Pigs have sensitive noses and are used in France to search for truffles which are underground fungi highly prized for use in cooking.

The outdoor system

On pig farms where farmers use the outdoor system, the pigs are tough outdoor breeds, such as black-and-white Saddlebacks, which produce very good meat. They are kept in grass paddocks, separated by hedges or fences. When the pigs have fed in one paddock for a while, they are moved on, and the field is then often used to grow cereals, as it is richly fertilized with pig manure. The sows give birth, or farrow, in farrowing huts in special farrowing paddocks.

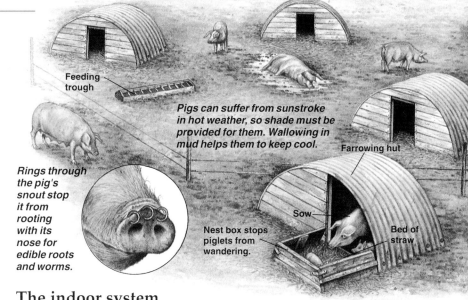

Feeding trough

Pigs can suffer from sunstroke in hot weather, so shade must be provided for them. Wallowing in mud helps them to keep cool.

Farrowing hut

Rings through the pig's snout stop it from rooting with its nose for edible roots and worms.

Sow

Nest box stops piglets from wandering.

Bed of straw

The indoor system

Many farmers specialize in raising pigs, and of these, many prefer to keep their animals inside fattening houses all the time, where they can carefully control food intake and temperature. This allows the farmers to concentrate on the large, white breeds such as Large Whites and Landraces, which produce excellent meat but don't like the damp and draughts of outdoor life.

Pig farmers with indoor systems generally use intensive farming methods, with their pigs being fed with special feeding machines, concentrated artificial foodstuffs and so on.

In a typical indoor system, pregnant sows are kept in separate small compartments called farrowing pens to prevent bullying and fighting. Weaned piglets are moved to the fattening house. This is a warm, well-ventilated building, with separate pens which keep the pigs in small groups and in dim light to reduce aggression.

A cut-away picture of a typical pig fattening house

The farmer can inspect the pigs from side passages.

Sloping floors carry the dung to the central passage.

Slats allow the dung to fall through into a pit.

Automatic food dispensers deliver food to each pen. If the food is dry, it may be dropped on the floor, but if wet, it goes into troughs.

Automatic drinking points supply water when the pig bites or pushes a nipple.

Trough

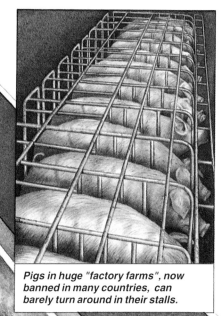

Pigs in huge "factory farms", now banned in many countries, can barely turn around in their stalls.

Poultry farming

Poultry, especially chickens, turkeys, ducks and geese, provide a major portion of the world's meat, as well as most of the billions of eggs that are eaten every year. Chicken eggs are most commonly eaten, but eggs of other poultry are also consumed. Chickens are by far the most important type of poultry, with more than 7,000 million kept around the world.

Free-range chickens

In developing countries, most farm families keep a few chickens for eggs and meat. The birds run free, scratching the earth for grass seeds, shoots and insects to eat. This "free-range" system is used by some poultry farmers in the developed world, but the eggs are expensive to produce.

Some free-range birds can roost (sleep) and lay their eggs where they like. Others are kept in large, open-air pens with a chicken house to provide shelter and a safe place for egg laying. They may be shut in at night if there are predators, such as foxes, around.

An open-air poultry pen

Chicken house (cut away)

Laying box - chickens enter from inside but eggs can be collected from outside.

Chickens' entrance ("pop hole")

Rhode Island Red chickens (a popular breed)

Feeder (may be put inside chicken house)

Energy for egg-laying

Laying eggs takes energy. Free-range hens use a lot of energy keeping warm and searching for food, so they only lay a few eggs. Hens kept warm and well-fed in battery units can put more energy into laying eggs, so they lay more. They average 240 eggs a year. Because free range hens need more space and food, and lay fewer eggs, the eggs cost more. Many people will pay for them, though, as they prefer the taste, or because they think the battery system is cruel.

Free-range egg

Free-range egg yolks have a deep orange shade, which comes from carotene, a pigment in the grass eaten by hens. The eggs taste richer and creamier than battery eggs.

Battery-produced egg

Poultry for the table

Chickens raised for meat are called broilers. They are kept in large numbers in heated buildings called broiler houses. Food and water are provided by automatic dispensers, and the birds grow quickly. With modern diets, they can reach 2kg (4½lb) in weight in six to seven weeks. It took almost twice that time 30 years ago. Most broilers are killed at this size, but some are fattened up to heavier weights and are killed at 14-16 weeks old.

A thick layer of wood shavings and chopped straw (the litter) covers the floor to soak up droppings in this chicken broiler house.

The building is well ventilated and regularly cleaned out and disinfected, so that the litter does not become damp or smelly. If it did, it would be likely to cause disease.

Turkeys

The main domestic breeds of turkey are the Broad-breasted Bronze, the Broad-breasted White and the White Holland. They are raised in grass paddocks or open-sided barns and fed on ground-up cereals with added vitamins. Depending on the breed, they can weigh between 3.5kg (7¾lb) and 22kg (48½lb) when mature. The heaviest breeds are fattened up for Christmas and Thanksgiving. They are killed at around six months old.

Ducks

Three-quarters of all domestic ducks are bred in Asia. They do much better than hens in the hot climate and are more resistant to diseases. The main meat breeds are the Pekin from China, the Rouen from France, the Aylesbury from England and the Muscovy from South America. The Khaki Campbell is the champion egg layer, with an average of more than 350 a year.

Geese

Geese are usually raised outdoors in "sets". Each set consists of a gander and four or five females. Unlike ducks, they do not need to be near water. The main breeds are the Toulouse from France and the Embden from northern Germany.

Broad-breasted bronze

White Holland

Pekin

Muscovy

Khaki Campbell

Aylesbury

Rouen

Toulouse

Embden

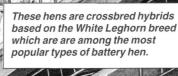

These hens are crossbred hybrids based on the White Leghorn breed which are are among the most popular types of battery hen.

The eggs roll into a tray and may be collected by a moving conveyor system.

Droppings fall into collecting trays below the cages, or onto a conveyor belt.

Food tray

Battery farming

Many specialist egg producers keep their hens in huge sheds, called battery units, which may contain up to 10,000 birds. They are kept in small wire cages, often stacked four tiers high, and fed from automatic dispensers on a special high-energy diet, with added minerals. The sheds are kept constantly warm, though in the tropics, open-sided sheds are used so the hens don't get too hot during the day.

Battery farming is very efficient, but some countries have banned it because they think the cramped conditions are cruel. Battery farmers say the hens are kept in perfect health and that it is the only way to produce enough eggs to meet the huge demand.

Mixed farming

Mixed farming is raising both crops and animals. The most basic type is found in developing countries, where families with tiny pieces of land produce just enough food to survive. In the developed world, farmers choose mixed farming if they have different types of land, such as some that is best suited to crops and some to raising livestock.

CROPS

MIXED FARMING

ANIMALS

Animal waste (manure) is used as a fertilizer.

Crops grown as food for animals. Crop waste, e.g. straw, is used for animal bedding, and some also for animal food.

Crops, meat, milk, eggs and wool are produced for food and for sale.

If demand for one product decreases, or a product fails, due to pests or diseases, the farmer has others to sell.

A typical mixed farm

A typical European mixed farm is between 20 and 50 hectares (50 and 125 acres) in area. It is run by a family, with two or three part-time helpers, and produces the family's food, plus surplus crops and livestock products for sale. In winter, the animals are fed on straw (dried grain plant stalks), hay (dried grass) or silage. Silage is a mixture of green crops such as grass, lucerne and clover, stored in the absence of air, so that it becomes "pickled" by the action of bacteria.

Key to European mixed farm

1. Pasture for livestock grazing

2. Grass grown for hay

3. Peas or beans grown as crops for sale or as fodder for livestock

4. 5. 6. Barley, oats and wheat - cereal crops grown for sale. They also provide straw for animal bedding and food in some cases.

7. Pigs fed on farm scraps

8. Ducks raised for meat

9. Farm buildings, e.g. house, barns for storage, sheds for animals and grain silos

10. Beehives. Bees raised to make honey for sale, and to pollinate beans and fruit trees.

11. Orchard for fruit crops

12. Poultry raised for eggs and meat

13. Root crops grown for sale (e.g. potatoes) or as fodder for livestock (e.g. turnips)

14. Kale grown as fodder

15. Woodland for timber and firewood

16. Greenhouses for growing seedlings

Crop rotation

If the same crop is grown each year on the same land, some nutrients in the soil get exhausted. Leaving a field fallow ("resting", with no crops) for a year allows nutrients to build up again, but this is expensive for farmers as they get no income from the field during that year. Many farmers overcome this problem by using artificial fertilizers on their land. However, a traditional crop rotation system is a much more natural way to replenish the soil, and still allows farmers to use all their land each year.

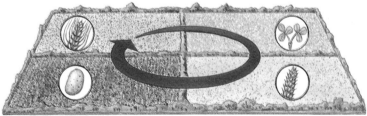

In the Norfolk rotation system, four main fields are used, which change crops in a four-year cycle.

Ist field - spring-planted barley grown as a cereal crop

2nd field - peas, beans or clover grown to replenish the soil. Bacteria in their roots take nitrogen from the air and pass it into the soil as vital plant nutrients such as nitrates. Sheep allowed to graze clover.

4th field - root crops, such as potatoes for market, or turnips for feeding livestock

3rd field - winter-planted wheat grown as a cereal crop

Agribusiness

Some mixed farms in the developed world produce food for the market using very efficient, modern business practices. These farms are known as agribusinesses. Many specialized farms that produce cereal crops or beef, for example, are run along the same lines. All these farms use intensive farming methods, with aids such as high-technology machines and artificial chemicals - plus highly sophisticated business techniques.

Fuel from waste

Rotting plant and animal waste can provide a useful gas, known as biogas. It is a mixture of methane (about 60%) and carbon dioxide (40%), and can be burned as a cooking gas, for example, or to heat farm buildings. Biogas is an increasingly important fuel in developing countries, where firewood is getting scarce. In China, more than 20 million people use it as cooking fuel.

Holding tank

Airtight tank called a digester, where plant and animal waste rot, producing biogas

Biogas passes to a gas holder.

Left-over material is collected to be used as fertilizer.

Slash and burn

Slash and burn is a traditional farming system which is used in the tropical forests of South America, Africa and Asia. Each farmer clears a small patch of forest and plants crops in the soil. This forest soil soon loses its fertility, so every few years the farmers have to move on and clear new patches of forest. These farmers are known as shifting culitivators, because they are constantly on the move. The term slash and burn describes how they prepare the fields for cultivation.

First the undergrowth and trees are cut down.

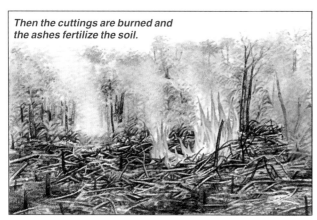

Then the cuttings are burned and the ashes fertilize the soil.

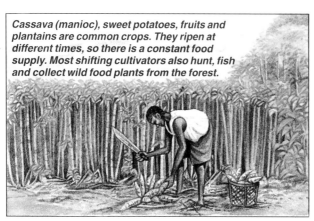

Cassava (manioc), sweet potatoes, fruits and plantains are common crops. They ripen at different times, so there is a constant food supply. Most shifting cultivators also hunt, fish and collect wild food plants from the forest.

In balance with nature

When shifting cultivators are well spread out, the system works well. Abandoned fields are often not used again for 30 years or more, giving the land time to recover. Forest seeds take root, and the small fields become a mass of vegetation. This slowly grows back into mature forest with the same rich variety of plants and animals as before.

This shows a small clearing which is beginning to recover after being abandoned. New seeds arrive from surrounding trees and the original plants grow back.

Why does the soil fail?

In the forest soils of most temperate regions, the layer containing humus is quite deep, giving a rich store of plant nutrients. By contrast, the tropical forest's nutrient store is mainly in the biomass - the living trees and other plants. Dead material on the ground decays very quickly in the hot, moist conditions, and the resulting nutrients are taken up just as quickly by the huge numbers of plants. So, few "spare" nutrients are stored in the soil. When a farmer burns off an area of forest, the ash adds nutrients to the soil but these are soon taken up by the crop plants. This causes the soil to become infertile and the farmer has to move on.

Soil in temperate forest

Soil in tropical forest

Storage of three plant nutrients in soil and in biomass of a temperate oak forest and a tropical forest.

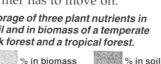

% in biomass   % in soil

Temperate oak forest			Tropical forest		
Nitrogen	Carbon	Magnesium	Nitrogen	Carbon	Magnesium

Destroying the forest

Unfortunately, there are now so many shifting cultivators that they are contributing to the destruction of the world's tropical forests. Loggers cutting down trees for timber and urban developers clearing land for building are also contributing to the destruction.

Huge areas of infertile land are now abandoned each year, but hardly any of the forest is left around them to provide the variety of new seeds which would allow the forest plants to grow again. Even if left alone, the land will still only acquire a covering of secondary forest. This is a type of forest made up of just a few species of pioneer plants - plants whose seeds can travel long distances on the wind and grow very quickly when they take root.

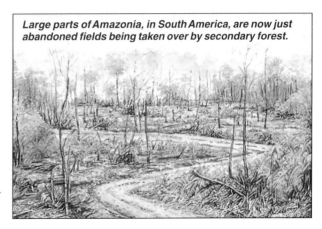

Large parts of Amazonia, in South America, are now just abandoned fields being taken over by secondary forest.

Losing the soil

Soil particles are held together by plant roots and by the humus in the soil. Because tropical forest soil is low in humus, the plant roots are vital. Where the forest is removed from hill slopes, great damage may be done in areas with heavy rains. Soil is swept into river valleys, leaving a surface of bare rock. This is called soil erosion.

Bare rocky crags in Madagascar, where the forest has been cleared

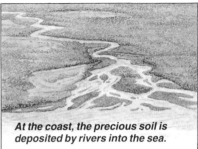

At the coast, the precious soil is deposited by rivers into the sea.

New ways of farming

People still need to live in the forest, so new farming systems are needed to enable them to produce food without damaging their environment. Most of these involve mixed farming of some kind, based on recycling resources and making better use of the natural forest products.

A typical small farm in an Asian forest, producing a steady supply of food at little cost.

Surrounding forest provides honey, fruit, wild game, rubber and other products which can be used locally or sold for cash.

Terracing allows crops to be grown on slopes without damaging the land.

Fodder crops provide food for animals while vegetable crops and fruit trees provide food for both the family and the animals.

Fast-growing trees supply animal fodder, and timber for housing and firewood, which is often scarce.

Chickens and pigs provide food and manure.

Artificial ponds stocked with fish provide food.

Animal droppings fall into the pond and fertilize water plants.

Pond weed provides food for the fish.

Pond mud, animal manure and crop waste are used to fertilize fields.

Cereal crops

About 15% of the world's farmland is used for growing cereals. These are types of grasses that are cultivated to produce large seeds called grains. They include wheat, barley, maize, rice, oats, millet and sorghum. Together they supply over half the food energy of the world's 5,500 million people. Cereal grains are rich in starch. Different types may be eaten as they are, or ground into a powder (milled) to make flour, which is the basis of many staple foods, such as bread and pasta, which form a large part of many people's diet. Cereal crops are also used to feed livestock and to make a variety of alcoholic drinks, such as beer and sake (rice wine).

This chart of world food production shows how dominant cereal crops are.

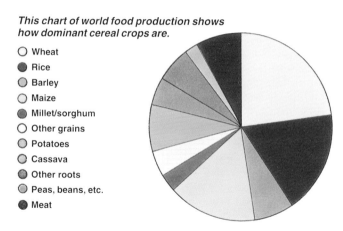

- ○ Wheat
- ● Rice
- ○ Barley
- ○ Maize
- ◐ Millet/sorghum
- ○ Other grains
- ○ Potatoes
- ○ Cassava
- ◐ Other roots
- ◐ Peas, beans, etc.
- ● Meat

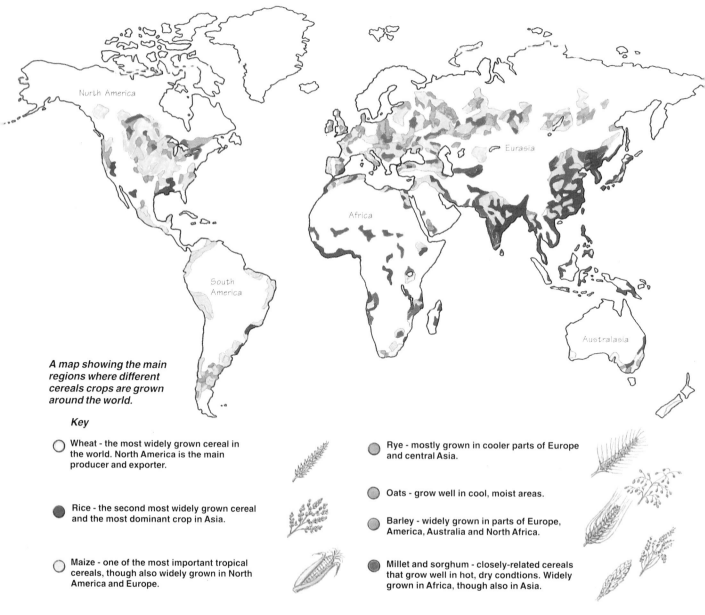

A map showing the main regions where different cereals crops are grown around the world.

Key

○ **Wheat** - the most widely grown cereal in the world. North America is the main producer and exporter.

● **Rice** - the second most widely grown cereal and the most dominant crop in Asia.

○ **Maize** - one of the most important tropical cereals, though also widely grown in North America and Europe.

◐ **Rye** - mostly grown in cooler parts of Europe and central Asia.

◐ **Oats** - grow well in cool, moist areas.

◐ **Barley** - widely grown in parts of Europe, America, Australia and North Africa.

● **Millet and sorghum** - closely-related cereals that grow well in hot, dry condtions. Widely grown in Africa, though also in Asia.

Cultivation and harvesting

Cereal plants are grown from grains kept from the previous harvest. The methods of sowing, cultivation and harvesting vary around the world, depending on factors such as the climate, the type of land and the level of technological development. In less developed countries, most tasks have to be done by hand, whereas in the developed world, intensive farming methods are often adopted using fertilizers and enormous machines such as combine harvesters.

Harvesting by hand. The plant stems with their grain clusters (heads) are cut using scythes, curved knives called sickles, or other types of knife. They may be stacked in bundles (stooks or sheaves) to dry and then in larger stacks called ricks, until threshed.

Scythe

Threshing separates the grain from the stalks (straw). The heads are beaten with flexible sticks or flails (two sticks hinged together), held and beaten against hard surfaces or trampled over by people or animals.

Flail

Tossing the threshed grain into the air from a sieve or tray allows the wind to blow away the chaff (outer seed cases) and other unwanted scraps. This is known as winnowing. Heavier waste is picked off the tray or separated off using the sieve holes.

Winnowing

In much of the developed world, combine harvesters do all the work. They cut and thresh the crop, blow out the chaff, deliver the grain into a truck, and dump the straw from a chute at the back.

In less developed countries, grain is sun-dried, then stored in jars, sacks or round clay or straw granaries on stilts. In the developed world, it is dried with warm air, and stored in concrete or metal silos up to 25m (82ft) high and 8m (26ft) in diameter.

Make your own bread

There are many different kinds of flour, milled from cereal crops, from highly purified white flour to wholemeal flour, which is milled with some of the grain seedcases left on. This is a recipe for bread, which uses wholemeal flour. Bread is made from a dough of flour and water. Yeast, a type of fungus, is used to make the dough rise. It breaks down the starch in the flour, making carbon dioxide gas.

INGREDIENTS

450g (3¾ US cups) wholemeal flour
2 tsp salt
2 tsp sugar
25g (2 tbs) melted margarine
15g (⅔ US cake) fresh yeast
or 2 tsp (one ¼ oz US package) dried yeast
300ml (1¼ US cups) tepid water

1. Mix the fresh yeast to a paste with the water (or add the dried yeast and sugar to about a cupful of the water and leave for about 10 minutes). Stir together the flour and salt (and sugar, if using fresh yeast) in a second bowl. Add the remaining water (if any), the yeast mixture and the melted margarine, and mix well to make a soft dough.

2. Turn out the dough onto a floured worktop, and knead it by pressing on it and squeezing it for about 10 minutes. Put it in a bowl in a warm place to rise, until it has doubled in size. Then knead it again, shape it into a loaf, sprinkle a little water or milk on the top, and put it on a well-greased baking sheet.

3. Bake your loaf at 230°C/450°F (gas mark 8) for 30 to 40 minutes.

Rice growing

Rice is probably the world's most important food crop. It is eaten every day by more than half of the world's population, and is particularly important in the poorer nations, because it can be grown cheaply in large quantities. Rice is rich in starch but low in protein and vitamins, so people who eat mainly rice need to balance their diet with a number of other foods, such as vegetables, fish, pork, duck meat and eggs.

Wet and dry rice cultivation

Rice is a grain or cereal crop. There are hundreds of varieties, and different types grow best in different conditions, so a farmer chooses his varieties according to his soil and climate. Types of rice that thrive in waterlogged soils are called paddy, or padi, and are widely grown in areas such as Asia and Central America, which have seasons of heavy rain, called monsoons. The farmers use a method of cultivation called the wet method, which uses flooded fields, known as paddy fields. Other varieties grow best in well-drained soils, for example in Australia and the US, and are grown like other cereals, using the dry method.

This scene shows a typical wet cultivation system in Asia, although ploughing has usually been completed by the time the seedlings are planted.

Paddy fields are separated by mud walls. They are ploughed using hand tools, or ox-drawn or buffalo-drawn ploughs, before being fully flooded. Weeds and stubble (the remains of the last crop) are ploughed in, and the earth is churned up.

The fields are flooded until there is at least 2cm (¾in) of water covering the land. Drainage channels, pumps and other devices are used to keep the water level stable.

New young plants, or seedlings, grown from seeds (rice grains) in nursery beds, are pressed into the mud in rows. The fields are weeded while they grow, and fertilizer may be added to the soil.

Major rice producers (Figures for 1990 in thousands of tonnes)

Oceania	923
Western Europe	2,265
E.E/USSR*	2,610
Near East	5,428
North America	7,027
Africa	9,285
Latin America	15,512
Far East	451,455

In Western Europe, each person eats on average about 3kg (6½lb) of rice in a year.

In Indonesia, each person eats that much in a week.

Year's supply - Western Europe

Year's supply - Indonesia

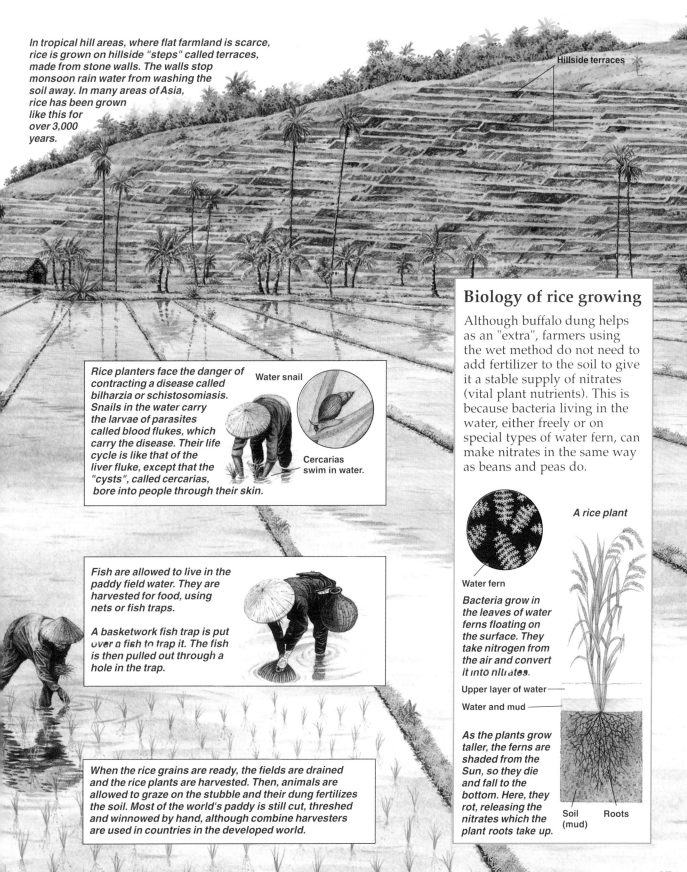

In tropical hill areas, where flat farmland is scarce, rice is grown on hillside "steps" called terraces, made from stone walls. The walls stop monsoon rain water from washing the soil away. In many areas of Asia, rice has been grown like this for over 3,000 years.

Hillside terraces

Biology of rice growing

Although buffalo dung helps as an "extra", farmers using the wet method do not need to add fertilizer to the soil to give it a stable supply of nitrates (vital plant nutrients). This is because bacteria living in the water, either freely or on special types of water fern, can make nitrates in the same way as beans and peas do.

Water fern

A rice plant

Bacteria grow in the leaves of water ferns floating on the surface. They take nitrogen from the air and convert it into nitrates.

Upper layer of water

Water and mud

As the plants grow taller, the ferns are shaded from the Sun, so they die and fall to the bottom. Here, they rot, releasing the nitrates which the plant roots take up.

Soil (mud)   Roots

Rice planters face the danger of contracting a disease called bilharzia or schistosomiasis. Snails in the water carry the larvae of parasites called blood flukes, which carry the disease. Their life cycle is like that of the liver fluke, except that the "cysts", called cercarias, bore into people through their skin.

Water snail

Cercarias swim in water.

Fish are allowed to live in the paddy field water. They are harvested for food, using nets or fish traps.

A basketwork fish trap is put over a fish to trap it. The fish is then pulled out through a hole in the trap.

When the rice grains are ready, the fields are drained and the rice plants are harvested. Then, animals are allowed to graze on the stubble and their dung fertilizes the soil. Most of the world's paddy is still cut, threshed and winnowed by hand, although combine harvesters are used in countries in the developed world.

Plantations

Plantations are areas planted with rows of trees or bushes which are perennial (long-lived). Plantations are most often monocultures - that is made up of one single crop. Plantations of crops such as tea, rubber, sugar cane and bananas are common in tropical areas, but temperate areas have plantations as well, such as timber plantations, vineyards and orchards.

A tropical plantation of pineapples, a crop which is grown for export to temperate countries.

The cash crop controversy

In many developing countries, much of the farmland is given over to plantations of export crops, or "cash crops" - crops such as tea, coffee and cotton grown for sale to rich countries. However, these rich countries keep the crop prices so low that the poor countries cannot earn enough to buy the things they need for their own people, such as fuel and food. Many people think that this system is unfair and the poor countries would be better off growing their own food, and also processing crops such as cotton in their own factories, providing both jobs and a better export product.

Alley cropping or intercropping is growing two crops in rows across a single field - either two cash crops or one cash crop and one crop for local consumption.

Growing bananas

Bananas came originally from Southeast Asia and were taken by missionaries to the Americas. Today, Ecuador in South America is the world's biggest producer. There are many different kinds of banana - yellow, red or green, long and thin or short and round. Some, like the plantain, can only be eaten once they are cooked. Cultivated bananas do not make seeds. New plants are grown from shoots from underground stems or roots, known as suckers, or from pieces of rhizomes, which are creeping stems that that run along the ground. The plants are pruned (cut back) each year, but produce fruit for about 20 years.

Bananas are harvested while still green. Each bunch is cut down with a machete or knife, often tied to the end of a long pole.

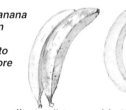

Cableways, powered by tractors, are often used to transport the bunches to the packing sheds.

Helping the ripening process

Bananas are refrigerated for export, so that they don't ripen too soon. Later, they are ripened with ethylene gas, pumped into storerooms or moving trucks. This really just helps nature, as ripe and ripening fruit produce this gas naturally, to cause ripening. You can use the gas from a ripe banana to ripen other fruit.

1. Take two unripe bananas, put one with a ripe banana or a ripe banana skin in a plastic bag and the other by itself in a second bag.

Ripe banana

Unripe bananas

2. Close the bags and put them in a warm place. After two or three days, have a look at them. The banana in the first bag should be ripening faster.

A ripe banana helps an unripe banana to ripen more quickly.

Ethylene affects all types of fruit. You could try this experiment using a ripe banana to ripen other fruit, such as green tomatoes.

A good bunch will weigh about 18kg (40lb) and have eight "hands", each of 15 bananas.

While still growing, bunches of bananas may be covered with bags to prevent damage by bats and other animals. The bags are kept on while the bananas are transported to the packing sheds.

Rubber plantations

Rubber is made from the milky sap, called latex, which comes from rubber trees. The original source of latex was the wild rubber trees in the forests of Brazil, but in the late 19th century some seeds were taken to Southeast Asia. Today, huge plantations in that region supply most of the world's rubber.

Lump of latex

Traditionally, the latex is "cured" by warming it over a fire. This process turns the latex into a hard, rubbery lump.

Tea plantations

There are huge plantations of tea bushes in China, India, East Africa, Japan, Indonesia and Russia. Only the tender young leaves at the tips of the branches are picked. These are crushed and dried before packing.

Tea bushes are pruned to about waist-height so that the pickers can reach the leaves easily.

Sugar cane

Sugar cane is originally from India, but most of the world's supplies now come from Central and South America. The plant stems (canes) are harvested each year and new canes grow from the stumps of the old ones. After harvesting, the canes are crushed to squeeze out the sugary juice. This is then filtered and boiled. As it cools, sugar crystals separate out from the liquid. In most cases, this sugar is refined (purified) by the country that buys it.

Sugar canes

A machine harvesting sugar cane. In some countries, it is still cut by hand.

In some places, such as Brazil, a lot of the cane sugar is used to make alcohol to use as car fuel. In Brazil, 3.5 million cars run on fuel containing 80% alcohol.

The "diesel trees"

In Brazil, there are plantations of special trees called copaibas. These produce an oily sap that can power a diesel engine. It is extracted from each tree once every six months. A large tree can yield as much as 20 litres (about 5 US gallons) in two hours.

Copaiba tree

Forestry

Forestry is the management and use of natural forests and also man-made forests, or plantations, to produce wood for a wide range of different uses. Hardwoods, such as oak and beech from temperate forests, and rosewood and mahogany from tropical areas, are used for furniture. Softwoods such as spruce, pine and fir are used for building or to make plywood, paper and cardboard. One of the main uses of wood in developing countries is for fuel.

Over 2,000 million people depend on wood for heating and cooking. Some have to walk miles each day for a few sticks.

Problems from the past

In the past, there were many more forests than there are now. Much of the forest which grew in temperate regions was lost centuries ago, but huge areas of tropical rainforest are still being destroyed by big logging companies who sell timber, and by people cutting down trees for fuel. This has left vast deforested areas with no trees. These areas are very vunerable to soil erosion, as there is no vegetation to protect the soil.

Uncontrolled logging has left parts of Madagascar scarred like a battlefield.

Modern forestry

Modern forestry is essentially tree farming. As with other farming, the idea is that harvesting one crop must be followed by planting and caring for the next, whether the forest is natural or man-made. Replanting protects soil and wildlife habitats in addition to providing wood. These diagrams shows three natural forestry systems.

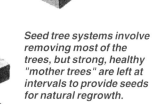

Clear felling involves taking all the trees from a small area. The surrounding trees provide seeds for new ones. New fast-growing types of tree may also be planted.

Seed tree systems involve removing most of the trees, but strong, healthy "mother trees" are left at intervals to provide seeds for natural regrowth.

Mother tree

Selective felling involves removing just a few trees at random, natural intervals. This is expensive, as it produces less wood, but it is especially useful in tourist areas as it doesn't spoil the scenery.

Natural tropical forestry

Large numbers of trees are still being felled in natural tropical forests and exported as a source of income. However, several countries have now adopted modern forestry systems. For example, in some areas, individual high-value trees, such as ebony and mahogany, are selected for felling, but at least one new seedling, sometimes of a faster-growing variety, is planted for each tree felled.

In many parts of Southeast Asia, elephants are still used to lift logs, and haul or roll them to areas where they can be loaded onto trucks.

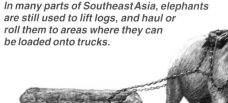

Plantation forestry

The demand for wood is still growing, so tree plantations are needed to add to the supply from natural forests. In Europe and North America, pine and other softwood plantations provide much of the wood used for building and making paper. Big softwood plantations are also being planted in some tropical countries to provide wood, so that the natural rainforests can be left alone.

Roads cut through a plantation allow harvesting machines in and loaded trucks out.

Plantations are usually planted in sections year by year so that the trees do not all mature at once. As each section is harvested, new seedlings are planted in the space.

This type of tree harvester is used for large trees. It has a flat circular saw which cuts off the trunk, and a rotating gripper arm which lifts the whole tree and lays it down.

Designer trees

Selective breeding is now used to create new varieties of trees. The new varieties can grow faster, are more resistant to diseases and produce more wood than unimproved trees.

Pollen from the male flowers of a selected "parent" plant is blown onto the female flowers of another "parent" using a puffer syringe. The female flowers are in clear bags to prevent accidental pollination by wind-blown pollen.

Once the seeds are mature, they are planted in nursery beds to produce "super-seedlings".

These two stems are both seven years old, but the improved variety on the left is twice as thick, which means that it contains four times as much wood.

Mountain forestry

On steep mountain slopes, harvested trees are cut into sections up to 10m (33ft) long. A steel cable, strung across a valley from a mobile tower, can be winched back and forth, dragging bundles of logs out of the felling area and up to a loading platform which is cut into the hillside.

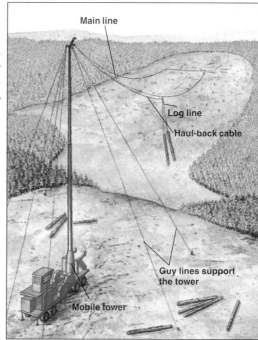

Main line

Log line

Haul-back cable

Guy lines support the tower

Mobile tower

Horticulture

Horticulture is the specialized cultivation of fruit, vegetables and ornamental plants. It is a form of intensive farming, which often uses fertilizers, pesticides, irrigation and greenhouses to achieve maximum yields. Vegetable and fruit growing is also called market gardening or truck farming. Horticultural units are often smaller than farms that grow main agricultural crops such as wheat, although in some countries, such as the Netherlands and Denmark, they may stretch over vast areas.

The rich soil and flat farmland of the Netherlands are ideal for growing flowers such as tulips and daffodils.

Vast areas of greenhouses and bulb fields grow millions of bulbs each year for sale, and the magnificent fields of bright flowers are also a tourist attraction.

Orchards

Apples, cherries, pears and plums are just some of the fruits grown in orchards (fruit tree plantations). Once, the trees in most orchards were tall, and fruit was harvested using ladders and baskets. Selective breeding has now produced smaller trees and bushes which are easier to manage. Top-quality fruit is still hand-picked, but much can now be done by machine.

Small trees planted in rows provide easy access for spraying and harvesting machines.

Vineyards

Wild grapes originated in western Asia and were being cultivated by 4,000 BC. Now they are grown in vineyards (grapevine plantations) wherever it is warm enough and not too wet. There are many varieties. Some are grown for eating, some for wine-making and some are dried to become currants, raisins and sultanas.

Workers picking grapes in a modern vineyard

On hillsides, most grapes are still harvested by hand. In flatter country, they can be harvested by machine.

Vines trained onto wires

Support wire

Plants are kept at the right height for picking grapes.

Controlled environments

Greenhouses, and plastic tunnels, called cloches, that are placed over crops in fields, are types of controlled environments. By creating artificial climates, they enable horticulturists to grow plants outside their normal growing seasons or far from their natural environments. They are expensive to run, so the growers concentrate on high-value produce such as tomatoes, strawberries, orchids or cacti.

Strawberries are grown out of season on Spanish hillsides inside rows and rows of plastic cloches. The plastic is supported inside by wire hoops.

Water comes from the rain, which soaks into the soil between the cloches, or from artificial drip irrigators.

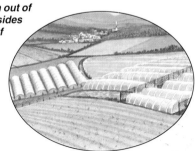

The greenhouse principle - the glass or plastic allows in the Sun's radiation, which warms the soil and plants.

The soil and plants give out heat radiation which has a lower energy level.

This cannot escape back out through the glass, so keeps the air warmer inside the greenhouse than outside.

Large modern commercial greenhouse

Ducts provide warm air heating when sunlight is not available or sufficient.

Air vents in walls and roof ensure good air circulation and cooling if necessary.

Automatic drip irrigation watering system with nutrients added to the water.

Farming without soil

A method of growing greenhouse plants without soil is known as hydroponics. It is being used increasingly, particularly where good soil is scarce. The plants are held upright in baskets by rods or wires, and given nutrients in their water supply, making soil unnecessary. The roots dangle straight into the nutrient liquid, or into a very loose material such as sand, gravel, cinders, a porous material called vermiculite, or specially-made porous ceramic pebbles.

Carnations growing in a hydroponic unit.

Grow a hydroponic lawn

Using hydroponics, you can grow a nutritious grass crop to use as food for rabbits, guinea pigs or cagebirds. In some countries, grass is grown this way to feed beef cattle. You will need a waterproof tray or a seedbox lined with plastic sheeting, a ready-made plant nutrient solution and a pad of capillary matting (from a garden store) or a clean piece of felt carpet underlay and a packet of grass seed.

1. Place the matting or felt underlay in the tray and sow the seed quite thickly over the surface.

Tray

Seeds   Matting

Jug

Nutrient solution

Cloth wick

2. Moisten the matting with the solution, making sure it is damp but not waterlogged. Set up an automatic feeder system, to keep the mat damp, by leading a cloth "wick" to the mat from a jug of the solution.

Damp matting

3. Put the tray and the jug in a dark place for a day or two to let the seeds germinate, then place in a warm light room. In 10-14 days you will have a crop you can simply peel off the mat. If you wash the mat it can be used again.

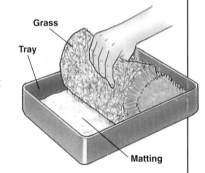

Grass

Tray

Matting

Irrigation

Irrigation is the artificial watering of farmland to allow crops to grow. It is needed in areas of very low rainfall and where there is a long dry season. Some desert countries, such as Egypt and Oman, are completely dependent on irrigation to grow food, but it is also used to increase crop production in many temperate regions of the world.

Even in deserts there is water below the ground, in rock layers called aquifers, which are saturated, or soaked, with water. It may come to the surface in springs, or wells may have to be dug.

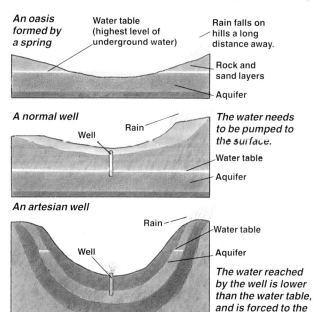

An oasis formed by a spring
Water table (highest level of underground water)
Rain falls on hills a long distance away.
Rock and sand layers
Aquifer

A normal well
Rain
Well
The water needs to be pumped to the surface.
Water table
Aquifer

An artesian well
Rain
Well
Water table
Aquifer
The water reached by the well is lower than the water table, and is forced to the surface by pressure.

Traditional irrigation

Traditional irrigation methods take water from natural springs or from wells. Spring water can be led straight to fields along channels, but well water must first be raised. This may be done by hand, using buckets, or by a variety of machines powered by people, electricity or animals.

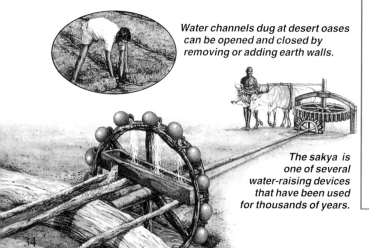

Water channels dug at desert oases can be opened and closed by removing or adding earth walls.

The sakya is one of several water-raising devices that have been used for thousands of years.

A model sakya

A sakya has pots set on a wheel. They scoop up water and pour it into a higher channel. To make a model, you will need an empty family-size ice cream tub (4 litres or 1 gallon), a knitting needle, a cork, some kitchen foil, a cardboard tube, seven cocktail sticks, a cap from a tube of toothpaste, some glue and some adhesive tape.

1. Cut seven 50mm (2in) x 50mm (2in) squares of foil. Press them around the cap to shape them into cups.

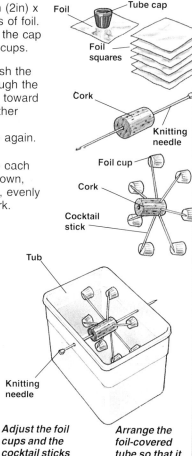

Foil
Tube cap
Foil squares
Cork
Knitting needle
Foil cup
Cork
Cocktail stick

2. Very carefully push the knitting needle through the cork (do not push it toward your hand or any other part of your body). Remove the needle again.

3. Glue a foil cup to each cocktail stick, as shown, and push the sticks, evenly spaced, into the cork.

4. Make holes with the knitting needle near the top of the tub, as shown, making them big enough for the needle to turn easily. Push the needle in through one hole, push the cork onto the needle and push the needle out the other side.

Tub
Knitting needle

5. Cut the tube in half lengthwise, cover one half in foil and cut the corner of the tub so you can tape this half in postion, as shown. Half fill the tub with water. Adjust the cork, cocktail sticks and cups so that when you rotate the needle between your fingers, the cups scoop water into the channel.

Adjust the foil cups and the cocktail sticks so that the cups scoop up the water.

Arrange the foil-covered tube so that it slopes slightly downward.

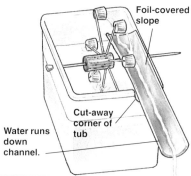

Foil-covered slope
Cut-away corner of tub
Water runs down channel.

Modern methods

Growing crops need a surprising amount of water. For example, about 10,000 tonnes (11,000 US tons) of it are needed to produce one tonne (1.1 US tons) of cotton. Modern intensive farming (see pages 36-37) makes use of highly mechanized water systems which allow huge areas to be irrigated. Most modern irrigation is done by pumping water into surface channels or by spraying directly onto the crops.

Spray units suspended from wheeled gantries can track across fields delivering a fine mist of water.

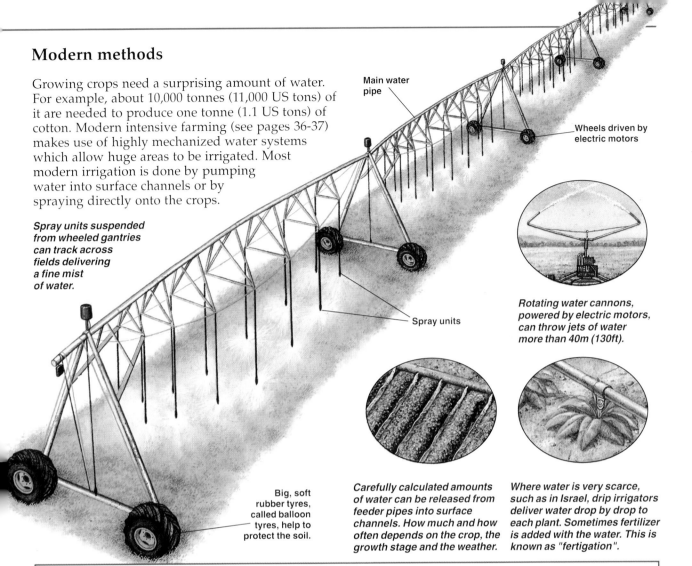

Main water pipe

Wheels driven by electric motors

Spray units

Rotating water cannons, powered by electric motors, can throw jets of water more than 40m (130ft).

Big, soft rubber tyres, called balloon tyres, help to protect the soil.

Carefully calculated amounts of water can be released from feeder pipes into surface channels. How much and how often depends on the crop, the growth stage and the weather.

Where water is very scarce, such as in Israel, drip irrigators deliver water drop by drop to each plant. Sometimes fertilizer is added with the water. This is known as "fertigation".

The hidden dangers

Irrigation brings its own problems. Unless it is very carefully controlled, with good drainage, the soil can become waterlogged - completely saturated, with no air spaces in it at all. Neither plants nor soil animals can live in these conditions. Also, in areas where evaporation rates are particularly high, irrigation and poor drainage can lead to mineral salts dissolved in the groundwater being carried up through the soil. The salts are then left either on or just below the soil surface. This forms rock-hard layers called salt pans in which no plants can grow.

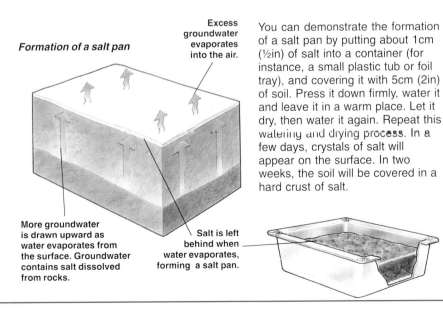

Formation of a salt pan

Excess groundwater evaporates into the air.

More groundwater is drawn upward as water evaporates from the surface. Groundwater contains salt dissolved from rocks.

Salt is left behind when water evaporates, forming a salt pan.

You can demonstrate the formation of a salt pan by putting about 1cm (½in) of salt into a container (for instance, a small plastic tub or foil tray), and covering it with 5cm (2in) of soil. Press it down firmly, water it and leave it in a warm place. Let it dry, then water it again. Repeat this watering and drying process. In a few days, crystals of salt will appear on the surface. In two weeks, the soil will be covered in a hard crust of salt.

Intensive farming

When farmers use high-technology machinery and farm chemicals, such as fertilizers and pesticides, to get the maximum amount of produce from their land, it is known as intensive farming. These methods can be used on small arable or livestock farms to increase yields, or on much larger farms, where they may be combined with up-to-date business practices to form agribusinesses. Farmers may adopt intensive methods if there is a demand for their produce and if they can afford the machinery and chemicals. Because intensive farming is expensive to set up and run, these methods are usually only practised in the richer countries.

Some farmers use high-tech machinery, such as helicopters, to spray fertilizers or pesticides on their crops.

Food mountains

Intensive farming uses expensive machinery and chemicals and produces very high yields. Farmers produce so much food that it can be sold more cheaply than food produced by traditional methods. This can lead to "mountains" of foods, such as wheat, beef or butter, or "lakes" of wine or oil, which cannot be sold. In some cases the surplus food is wasted. While this is happening in some developed countries, in other parts of the world people are starving.

A food mountain of grain stored in a warehouse. It may have to be destroyed.

Farm energy needs

Intensive farming methods use a vast amount of energy, not just for heating buildings, but also for running farm machinery. Energy is also used in manufacturing the chemicals that are used on farms. In contrast, on traditional farms, much of the energy comes from human labour and from natural fertilizers such as animal manure. With modern machines, just two people can easily work a 400 hectare (988 acre) arable farm.

Without access to machines, a whole family has to work full-time to run a two hectare (five acre) farm in Africa or Asia.

New animal and crop varieties

Selective breeding allows farmers to produce high-quality plants and animals, but a further step in the development of new improved species is called genetic engineering. Scientists have discovered methods of isolating the chemicals, called genes, that carry specific information from one generation to the next. For instance, they have implanted genes that act like pesticides, giving a plant built-in resistance to insect pests. They have also produced genes that delay the ripening of fruit.

These genetically engineered tomatoes have been developed to ripen slowly, making them easier to store and transport.

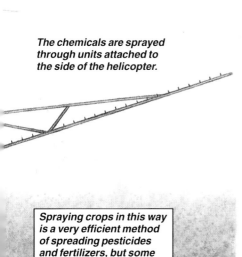

The chemicals are sprayed through units attached to the side of the helicopter.

Spraying crops in this way is a very efficient method of spreading pesticides and fertilizers, but some may be carried by the wind and affect other areas.

Using pesticides

Throughout the world, nearly a third of all crops are damaged by animal or insect pests, diseases, fungi and weeds. Many farmers in developed countries use a wide range of pesticides to protect their crops. They use insecticides to fight insect pests, herbicides to kill weeds and fungicides for moulds.

On many modern farms, crops are sprayed from tractor-drawn units that can aim the chemicals where they will be most effective.

Poison in the food chain

Some pesticides have long-lasting effects. One such type is DDT, once used widely around the world. Insects that live on crops treated with DDT are eaten by small birds, which in turn are eaten by larger birds, such as hawks. Tragically, these birds end up with a fatal or damaging dose of DDT as it gets passed along the food chain and is stored in animal body fat.

Meat eater (e.g. peregrine)

Warbler (insect eater)

Ladybird (insect eater)

Aphids (plant eater)

A DDT food chain

Grain treated with DDT

The danger of DDT was discovered in the 1960s when peregrines failed to breed. The pesticide which had built up in their bodies made their eggshells so brittle that, when the birds sat on the eggs, the shells broke.

Using fertilizers

Intensive farming can only produce such high yields by using artificial fertilizers. Fertilizers replace elements such as nitrogen, which the crops take out of the soil.

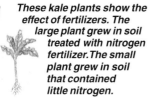

These kale plants show the effect of fertilizers. The large plant grew in soil treated with nitrogen fertilizer. The small plant grew in soil that contained little nitrogen.

The dangers of fertilizers

Some fertilizer gets washed into lakes where it causes rapid growth of tiny plants called algae. When the algae die, they are recycled by bacteria, but this process uses up the oxygen in the water, resulting in the death of other plants and animals.

Algae in a stream which has been polluted by fertilizers.

Is your stream polluted?

Lack of oxygen can be caused by industrial pollution as well as by fertilizers. You can tell if a stream is healthy or starved of oxygen by looking at the creatures that live in it. To do this you will need a large, plastic container such as a bottle or bucket, some small, clear plastic bottles and a magnifier.

ALWAYS TAKE GREAT CARE NEAR WATER, AND DO NOT GO ALONE.

1. Carefully collect a sample of water from the stream in your large plastic container.

2. Transfer a quantity of the water into some of your bottles. Use the magnifier to study the creatures in each sample.

In heavily polluted water you will find few animals apart from:

Sludge worms (*Tubifex*)

Bloodworms (midge larvae)

Rat-tailed maggots (fly larvae)

In less polluted water you will find those animals plus:

Pond snails

Water slaters

In clean water you will find all these animals plus:

Caddis-fly larvae

Mayfly larvae

Freshwater shrimps

Organic farming

Producing crops and livestock without using chemicals is known as organic farming. In developing countries this is the traditional way of farming, but it is now being reintroduced in many countries where intensive methods have become widespread. This is due to concerns about the amount of chemicals and energy used in intensive farming. Natural methods do not involve costly fertilizers, but the produce still tends to be expensive. This is because natural farming is labour-intensive and does not produce large quantities that can be sold cheaply.

Fruit and vegetables grown using organic methods are expensive, but people still choose to buy them.

Improving soils naturally

Organic farming methods make no use of man-made chemicals to improve soil quality. Traditionally, soil is kept fertile by adding animal manure and other organic matter, such as compost. After two or three years of growing crops the field is left fallow for a year and grazing animals fertilize it with their droppings. Other methods, such as crop rotation (see page 21), are also used to replace nutrients in the soil. Some farmers grow plants such as mustard and red clover, which are known as "green manures". These are dug back into the soil to provide humus and nutrients.

Improving soils

Crops grown in soil that is deficient in plant nutrients often suffer from poor growth and low yields. This is often a problem in tropical countries. One answer would be to add chemical fertilizers to the soils, but this is too costly in developing countries. A natural way to improve the soil is to grow plants of the pea and bean family which replenish soil with nutrients and provide food for people and animals.

In some rubber plantations, beans are grown beneath the rubber trees to improve the soil.

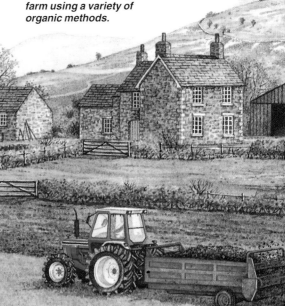

This scene shows a typical farm using a variety of organic methods.

Manure from pig pens and chicken houses is used as a natural fertilizer as it is rich in nitrogen, phosphorus and potassium.

Hand rotovators are used to break up the soil and turn in manure or compost.

As the shredders in a muck spreader rotate, they break up the manure and fling it out of the back.

Many farmers grow a variety of produce for themselves, but some crops, such as kale, can be grown for fodder, as well as for sale.

Small fields are enclosed by hedges which provide a natural habitat for many birds and insects.

Make a compost heap

If you have access to a garden, you can build your own compost heap which will turn garden and kitchen waste into a useful fertilizer. It will take a few months to work, but you can watch how the heap changes and how small animals help in the composting process. You will need organic waste from the garden, such as grass cuttings, leaves and weeds, and kitchen refuse, such as tea leaves and vegetable peelings, but not meat scraps. You will also need some thick sticks, twelve bricks or several logs.

1. If possible choose a spot hidden from view and protected from wind and rain. Build a platform for the heap by placing the bricks or logs in four rows, then put the sticks at different angles across them to form a grid.

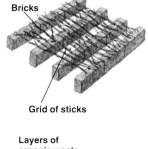

Bricks

Grid of sticks

2. Build up the compost heap with 15-20cm (6-8in) layers of organic waste. Separate each layer with a 2.5cm (1in) layer of soil.

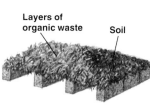

Layers of organic waste

Soil

3. Continue to add layers of waste and soil. A heap started in spring or early summer will produce a dark brown, crumbly compost in about three months. One started in the winter will compost more slowly and may take about six months.

As you build up the compost heap, try to keep the sides straight and pick up any bits which fall.

4. Over the months, lift up the layers occasionally with a garden fork and you may see some of the wildlife that helps in the composting process.

Ants, centipedes and spiders hunt among the rotting debris.

Woodlice, springtails and millipedes feed on rotting plant material.

As the heap turns to compost, small striped worms called brandlings appear, along with small white potworms.

Biological pest control

Organic farmers do not use pesticides to protect their crops, but instead use a variety of natural methods. This is known as integrated pest management. Some farmers plant rows of onions among their crops. The strong smell of the onions keeps pests away.

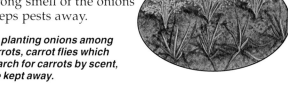

By planting onions among carrots, carrot flies which search for carrots by scent, are kept away.

Another natural method of pest control is to introduce an insect to a crop which does not harm it, but feeds on an insect which does. For instance, silverleaf whitefly cause millions of dollars worth of damage to melons, oranges and lemons in California each year. Scientists are experimenting with a small brown beetle which eats whitefly and which they hope will control the pests.

In Asia, some farmers place strips of bamboo between maize plants to allow predatory ants to climb onto the plants. The ants eat the pests that damage the maize.

Organic husbandry

Farmers who raise livestock by organic methods choose hardy breeds which do not need expensive heated sheds. The animals are fed on silage and fodder crops grown on the farm and are not given chemical food additives.

Scottish Highland cattle can live outdoors all year round.

Conserving the land

Human activities can have a devastating effect on the land. Where too many people cut down trees, use slash and burn farming techniques or graze too many animals on sparse vegetation, the plant covering is removed, allowing the fragile topsoil to be stripped away by the wind and rain. This soil erosion must be prevented if food is to be grown on the land.

Terrible famines result from soil erosion. Many thousands of people have to leave their homes in search of food, such as that given out at this UN feeding station.

Stabilizing the hills

Some of the worst soil erosion of all occurs on hillsides, especially in areas with heavy rains. Terraces and walls are built on hillsides to prevent soil from being washed away.

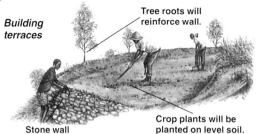

Building terraces

Tree roots will reinforce wall.

Crop plants will be planted on level soil.

Stone wall

Bunds are curved walls built from stones. Soil washed downhill collects behind them to form mini-terraces.

Crops can be planted here.

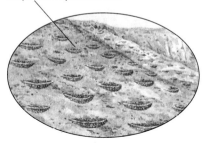

Stone walls are often built across gullies, as in this pine plantation. They prevent a rush of water from eroding the hillside during heavy rains.

Stone wall

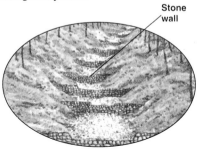

Holding back the desert

In North Africa, overgrazing has turned vast areas into desert, leaving less and less grazing land. Sand dunes moved by wind now threaten the farmland that remains. Tough grasses, brushwood fences, and fast-growing trees are all being used to hold back the desert.

Criss-crossed fences stop desert sand from moving any farther. Fast-growing trees will yield timber, firewood and fodder for animals. Tree roots and tough, long-rooted grasses help to anchor the sand.

Soil conservation model

This model shows how quickly soil is eroded by rainfall when there is no protective plant cover. You will need a 1,600mm x 250mm (63in x 10in) piece of hardboard or plywood, a ruler, some tough string, a small saw, scissors and strong adhesive tape, a 4mm (⅛in) drill, some sheets of kitchen film, a small sharp pin, (such as a map pin), two large plastic drinks bottles (one with a flat-topped lid), six jars of the same size and some grass or cress seed.

1. Mark out the hardboard sheet as shown, then use the saw to cut along the dotted lines to make the six rectangles, three diamond shapes and one triangle. You will find that you have two pieces of wood that are not used. Carefully cut the corners off the diamond shapes and drill all the holes that are marked on the diagrams below. Make sure that you observe all the proper safety precautions when you are sawing and drilling.

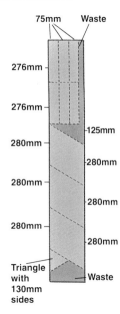

75mm   Waste

276mm

276mm

125mm

280mm

280mm

280mm

280mm

280mm

280mm

Triangle with 130mm sides

Waste

If you want to use imperial measurements, replace the millimetre measurements as shown here:

65mm - 2½in

75mm - 3in

125mm - 4½in

130mm - 5in

276mm - 10¾in

280mm - 11in

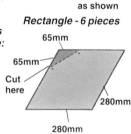

276mm

75mm

Drill holes as shown

Rectangle - 6 pieces

65mm

65mm

Cut here

280mm

280mm

Diamond - 3 pieces

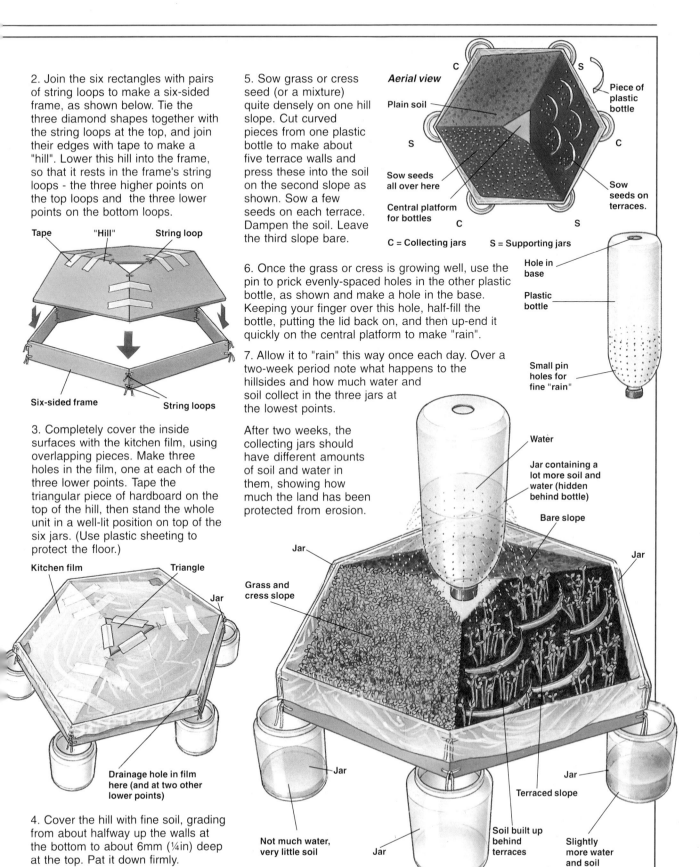

2. Join the six rectangles with pairs of string loops to make a six-sided frame, as shown below. Tie the three diamond shapes together with the string loops at the top, and join their edges with tape to make a "hill". Lower this hill into the frame, so that it rests in the frame's string loops - the three higher points on the top loops and the three lower points on the bottom loops.

Tape

"Hill"

String loop

Six-sided frame

String loops

3. Completely cover the inside surfaces with the kitchen film, using overlapping pieces. Make three holes in the film, one at each of the three lower points. Tape the triangular piece of hardboard on the top of the hill, then stand the whole unit in a well-lit position on top of the six jars. (Use plastic sheeting to protect the floor.)

Kitchen film

Triangle

Jar

Drainage hole in film here (and at two other lower points)

4. Cover the hill with fine soil, grading from about halfway up the walls at the bottom to about 6mm (¼in) deep at the top. Pat it down firmly.

5. Sow grass or cress seed (or a mixture) quite densely on one hill slope. Cut curved pieces from one plastic bottle to make about five terrace walls and press these into the soil on the second slope as shown. Sow a few seeds on each terrace. Dampen the soil. Leave the third slope bare.

6. Once the grass or cress is growing well, use the pin to prick evenly-spaced holes in the other plastic bottle, as shown and make a hole in the base. Keeping your finger over this hole, half-fill the bottle, putting the lid back on, and then up-end it quickly on the central platform to make "rain".

7. Allow it to "rain" this way once each day. Over a two-week period note what happens to the hillsides and how much water and soil collect in the three jars at the lowest points.

After two weeks, the collecting jars should have different amounts of soil and water in them, showing how much the land has been protected from erosion.

Aerial view

Plain soil

Sow seeds all over here

Central platform for bottles

C = Collecting jars   S = Supporting jars

Piece of plastic bottle

Sow seeds on terraces.

Hole in base

Plastic bottle

Small pin holes for fine "rain"

Water

Jar containing a lot more soil and water (hidden behind bottle)

Bare slope

Jar

Jar

Grass and cress slope

Jar

Terraced slope

Jar

Not much water, very little soil

Jar

Soil built up behind terraces

Slightly more water and soil

Unusual livestock farming

Crocodiles, moths and antelopes may not sound like farm animals to many people, but these and many other animals can be reared and managed to produce food and other products. In some situations these sorts of species can be farmed more efficiently and profitably than "normal" livestock such as pigs, sheep and cows. In a number of cases this kind of farming can even help to protect species that are endangered in the wild.

In some parts of Europe and North America, where they are naturally equipped to survive in the conditions, red deer are farmed for their meat, which is called venison.

Fish farming

Farming fish, especially carp, in natural and man-made ponds, is an ancient practice in China, and supplies about 40% of the fish eaten there. Trout farms and salmon farms are a more recent invention but are now common in both Europe and North America. Other species, such as tilapia in South America and milkfish in the Philippines, are now being farmed in many developing countries and helping to increase food supplies.

A modern trout farm

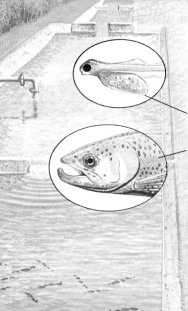

Fertilized eggs are hatched in nursery tanks and then the fish are moved through a series of ponds or tanks as they grow. Here a river has been diverted to create a series of ponds.

Hatchling (called an alevin)

The trout reach marketable size after about 18 months. Some are kept back to breed the next generation.

Salmon (saltwater fish) are now farmed. They are hatched in fresh water, but later moved to cages in sea inlets and bays as shown below.

Ostrich farming

Ostriches are farmed in herds in South Africa. The adult birds are caught every 8-9 months and their feathers are "harvested" to make fashion accessories and feather dusters. Ostriches also provide leather and meat in some countries, and their enormous eggshells are sold to tourists as souvenirs.

Young ostriches like to stay in groups, which make them easier to manage.

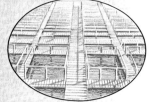

When harvesting ostrich feathers, a crush pen stops the bird from kicking and a hood keeps it quiet. Enough feathers are left to protect the bird from sunstroke. The adult male's black and white feathers are the most valuable.

Crocodile farms

By the 1960s, many of the world's crocodiles and alligators had been almost wiped out by hunters. Now they are farmed and this produces meat and skins for sale as well as creating jobs for local people. Some young animals are also put back in the wild from each new generation, to replace the animals that are still killed by poachers.

Saltwater crocodiles are farmed for their skins and meat in Southeast Asia and Australia.

Silk moth farming

Over 85% of the world's silk comes from the cocoons spun by the larvae (young forms) of *Bombyx mori* moths. In each generation, a few moths are allowed to hatch out and become breeding adults. The rest are killed while they are still inside their cocoons which are then treated so that the silk can be wound onto spools.

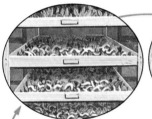

Moth eggs hatch into larvae (silkworms) on trays of mulberry leaves, which are their food.

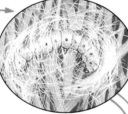

After four to six weeks the silkworms stop feeding, crawl into a nest of straw and spin their cocoons.

These adults are allowed to hatch. They will breed, and the females will produce the next batch of eggs.

The cocoons are softened in hot water, then the silk is unwound. Each cocoon produces a single strand up to 280m (920ft) long. Groups of eight strands are combined by machine to make silk threads.

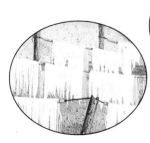

Skeins of silk threads drying in the sun

Game ranching

In many parts of the world, wild game animals, such as eland, are raised on ranches for meat and other products. These native species are often more resistant to local diseases than "foreign" cattle or sheep. They are also better adapted to the climate, and can use the available food efficiently and without damaging the environment.

Some game species now farmed (these pictures are not to scale).

Hippopotamus (Uganda)

Saiga antelope (central Asia)

Capybara (South America)

Wildlife safaris

On many game ranches, the farmed animals mix with the wild animals in the area, even though this means that some are killed by predators. The farmers allow this because they can then offer wildlife safaris. Tourists pay to travel around the ranches to photograph the wild animals (and even hunt a carefully managed number each year). This provides money for the farm upkeep, and extra jobs for the people, as guides or drivers.

Tourist safaris can generate large amounts of income for farmers.

Typical open-topped tourist bus

The wildlife can be photographed from very close up, as the animals are used to the buses.

Feeding the world

Around the world, one person in every ten is permanently hungry. Every year over 40,000 children die from hunger or from diseases related to hunger and poor diet. More than enough food is produced each year to feed all the people in the world, but much of the food is in the wrong place. While people starve in parts of Asia and Africa, some farmers in North America and Europe are producing so much, that food is wasted.

Soaring population

The population of the world is more than 5,500 million and it is thought that by the year 2000 it may exceed 6,000 million. At the present rate, the world's population is increasing by 80 million people every year, and all these people need food to eat.

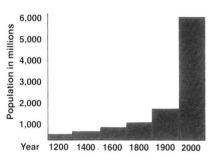

Fair shares?

Europe has one quarter of the world's population, but produces almost half the total supply of food. At the other extreme, in the Far East, about 40% of the world's population survives on just 14% of the total food available.

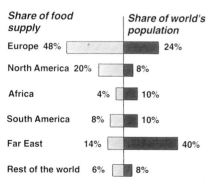

Share of food supply	Share of world's population
Europe 48%	24%
North America 20%	8%
Africa 4%	10%
South America 8%	10%
Far East 14%	40%
Rest of the world 6%	8%

Problems of land use

Only about 11% of the Earth's surface is used for producing food. The remaining areas are largely unsuitable for growing crops or supporting livestock, mainly because they are too cold or too dry for farming. Overgrazing and soil erosion have also resulted in areas of land being made too poor to grow crops and fodder successfully.

This map shows land use around the world.

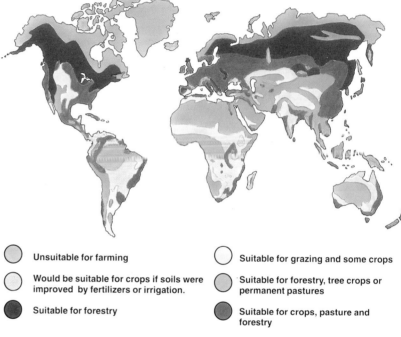

⬤ Unsuitable for farming	◯ Suitable for grazing and some crops
◉ Would be suitable for crops if soils were improved by fertilizers or irrigation.	◉ Suitable for forestry, tree crops or permanent pastures
⬤ Suitable for forestry	⬤ Suitable for crops, pasture and forestry

Distributing food

One short-term solution to food shortages is for countries that produce food mountains (see page 36) to send food to countries where people are starving. But this is not as easy as it sounds. Although some products, such as grain and dried milk, can be stored and shipped easily, fresh food such as vegetables, meat and dairy products need to be preserved and transported in refrigerators, which the poorer countries do not possess. Also, shipping and distribution have to be paid for and many of the countries where food is most needed cannot afford to do this.

Grain being unloaded at a quay, ready for distribution. It is expensive to transport food in bulk. Money has to be found to pay for ships, trucks, fuel and manpower.

Food aid

Natural disasters, such as floods, droughts, hurricanes or crop diseases, may devastate farmland and cause severe food shortages. In areas where food is always scarce, disasters like these may lead to famine. Food shortages may also occur when wars stop food from being distributed. During emergencies, various international aid organizations and United Nations agencies provide emergency food aid for war or disaster victims.

Food and medical supplies being transported by an aid organization during a famine in Sudan.

Fighting pests

Cassava is a major food source for 80% of the population of Africa. During the 1970s, however, an insect pest, the cassava mealybug, was accidentally introduced into Africa. The pests spread rapidly, damaging and destroying massive areas of crops. Chemical pesticides were too expensive for farmers to use, but scientists discovered that a species of wasp preyed on the mealybug. Several international aid organizations provided money for the large-scale distribution of the wasps and the amount of affected crops has gradually declined.

Mealybugs feeding on a cassava plant.

Wasps, like this one, prey on the cassava mealybugs.

Long-term aid

In an effort to help farmers produce greater quantities of food in areas where food is scarce, international aid organizations support a large variety of different types of farming projects. They help by providing funds and expertise in projects such as digging wells, developing agricultural and forestry systems and designing and building irrigation systems. They also provide tools, farming equipment, fertilizers, pesticides and varieties of seed that have been selectively-bred to produce high yields. They also encourage long-term improvements in water supplies, hygiene, health care and education.

A WaterAid project in villages in Tamil Nadu in India, helped to improve water supplies by installing handpumps to wells.

Wells are covered to protect them from contamination and from insects which breed in the water and spread diseases.

Local women were trained so they could repair and maintain the pumps without the need for outside help.

As well as providing clean drinking water, excess water is used to cultivate fruit trees such as coconut, papaya and banana.

Glossary

Agribusiness. The practice of farming as a large-scale business enterprise, using up-to-date business techniques and high-technology machinery.

Agriculture. The precise, scientific term for farming in all forms - from large-scale **cultivation** to the raising of animals.

Arable farming. Farming that concentrates on the growing of crops. Arable land is suitable for **cultivation** (as opposed to pasture land or woodland).

Artificial insemination (**AI**). The insertion of sperm (male reproductive cells), collected in a tube from a male animal, into a female animal by human hand for purposes of **breeding**.

Battery units. Very cramped **poultry** cages, stacked in long rows as part of a battery farm (a poultry **factory farm**). Now banned in many countries.

Biogas. Gas, mainly methane, produced by rotting waste and dung. It can be used as a fuel.

Breed. Each different type of plant or animal within a species is called a breed - for example, a Merino sheep as distinct from a Dalesbred sheep.

Breeding. The production of new young plants or animals - farmers must make sure their animals breed successfully.

Cash crops. Crops grown specifically because they can be exported in order to bring in money.

Cereals. A group of related grasses cultivated for their grains (large seeds) which grow in clusters (heads) at the top of their stalks. The grains are ground to produce flour.

Colostrum. The special milk, rich in antibodies, that a female mammal produces for her young for a brief period after it is born and before her normal milk starts to flow.

Crop rotation. The growing of different crops in a field in successive years, so as to replenish the soil with its vital **plant nutrients**.

Crossbreeding. The creation of a new **breed** of animal or plant by using parents of different breeds.

Cultivation. The science of managing soil and plants in order to grow crops to feed people or domestic animals.

Deforestation. The loss of tree cover from an area of land, due to various causes, for instance excessive logging or pollution such as acid rain.

Desertification. The transformation of otherwise productive land into desert, due to **soil erosion**.

Extensive farming. The spreading out of **livestock** or crops over large areas of land due to sparse natural vegetation for grazing or poor soil quality for **cultivation**.

Factory farming. Keeping **livestock** in cramped, factory-style conditions, with a high degree of automation (feeding machines, etc.), in order to produce meat in the most efficient and cost-effective way, and in the quantities required by today's growing population. Now generally regarded as cruel and banned in many countries.

Fertilizer. Any substance which helps to replenish **plant nutrients** in the soil, and so make the soil fertile (able to sustain life). Fertilizers range from animal dung to powdered chemicals.

Food mountains. A term used to describe surplus food which cannot be sold and is often wasted. It is often the result of **intensive farming**.

Forestry. The management of natural forests and tree **plantations** in order to **harvest** trees for their wood.

Genetic engineering. A scientific process which involves implanting genetic material into a species of plant or animal in order to produce a specific improvement, which will be passed on to the next generation.

Germination. The emergence of a new young plant from a seed.

Harvesting. The collection of the season's ripe crop, such as grain, fruit or roots, from cultivated plants.

Horticulture. Literally means "gardening". In farming terms, the science of growing, processing and marketing fruits, vegetables and ornamental plants.

Humus. The rotted mixture of plant and animal remains which binds soil together and provides many of the vital **plant nutrients**.

Husbandry. The science of **breeding** and keeping animals to provide milk, meat, skins and transportation or animal power for people. The animals are known as **livestock**.

Hydroponics. Growing plants without soil, by supplying the physical support, water and **plant nutrients** they need.

Integrated Pest Management (IPM). Any system in which a farmer uses a variety of different methods to protect crops from pest damage, for example, **crop rotation** and encouragement of predators that destroy insect pests.

Intensive farming. Making the best use of every small piece of land and producing the maximum amount from the land available.

Irrigation. The artificial watering of the land in dry areas or at times of low rainfall, in order to grow crops or increase crop production.

Livestock. Animals raised on a farm for their wool, hide, milk or eggs, or for their meat, or to be used as work animals.

Monoculture. An area of **cultivation** of one type of plant only.

Monsoon. A wind which blows from different directions at different times of the year, creating a wet or rainy season, followed by a dry season. The wet and dry seasons themselves are often also known as monsoons.

Nitrates. Chemical compounds that contain nitrogen (an important **plant nutrient**). Natural nitrogen **fertilizers** include animal manure, guano (bird droppings) and sodium nitrate, which can be mined in some countries. Most farmers now use synthetic (man-made) nitrogen fertilizers.

Organic farming. Farming which does not use any artificial chemicals, such as **fertilizers** and **pesticides**, to produce crops or **livestock**.

Overgrazing. Putting too many animals on a piece of land, with the result that the vegetation is destroyed, leaving the soil exposed to **soil erosion**. Overgrazing is a major cause of **desertification** in parts of Africa.

Paddy (padi). Varieties of rice plant which thrive in waterlogged soil. The fields they are grown in are known as paddy fields.

Parasites. Organisms (plants or animals, often microscopic) which live in or on other organisms, and live by feeding off them.

Pesticides. Chemicals used by farmers and gardeners to kill pests which harm their plants.

Photosynthesis. The process by which plants make their own simple food (glucose), by using the energy of sunlight to cause a reaction between the gas carbon dioxide and water.

Plantations. Areas of trees or bushes, farmed for their produce, such as bananas, coffee or rubber in tropical areas, and grapes, apples and pears in temperate areas. Trees are also farmed in plantations for their wood (see **Forestry**).

Plant nutrients. The essential substances which a plant needs to live and grow. Among these are various minerals, and compounds of nitrogen called **nitrates**.

Poultry. Domestic fowl, for example chickens, turkeys and ducks, that are reared for their meat, eggs or feathers.

Pure breeding. The creation of a new plant or animal of the same **breed** as its parents, by mating parents of the same **breed**.

Salt pan. A hard layer of salt or other minerals, which forms on or just below the surface of the land, making it infertile. It results from evaporation of water from waterlogged land, which is often caused by inadequate drainage.

Secondary forest. Forest composed of just a few types of trees and bushes. These are the only ones able to recolonize the huge tracts of land left after the large-scale destruction of primary forest, which has a much greater variety of plants and animals.

Selective breeding. The manipulation of plant or animal **breeding** by humans, in order to produce specific, chosen results, e.g. **crossbreeding**.

Silage. Animal fodder made from cut grass and other greenstuff, such as clover and lucerne, which has been allowed to "pickle" or become acidic, by storing it in the absence of air.

Slash and burn (shifting cultivation). A simple farming method. It involves clearing small patches of forest, growing crops on the land for short periods until the soil is exhausted, then moving on to clear new patches.

Soil erosion. The removal of soil, by wind or water, which occurs after land has lost the plants which grow on it. There are no longer roots to help bind the soil, nor is there the binding **humus** inside it. It becomes loose and is easily removed, leaving barren rock.

Starch. The form in which plants store glucose, the simple food they make by **photosynthesis**. People **harvest** many plant crops, such as cereal grains, potatoes and cassava, for the starch they contain.

Terracing. A way of making use of sloping land for farming. Low walls are built to create a series of "stepped" fields down the slope. They prevent soil from being washed away by rain.

Threshing. Beating or trampling on harvested **cereal** crops to remove the grains from the stalks.

Weaning. Removing a young animal from access to its mother's milk, and beginning to feed it on solid food.

Winnowing. Further sorting of the grains of a **cereal** crop after **threshing**. The grains are separated from loose husks and other waste matter (small pieces of stalk, etc.) which may have been collected up with them.

Acknowledgements

The publishers are grateful to the following people and organizations for the provision of information and materials for use as artists' reference:

Ford New Holland Ltd: combine harvester - front cover and page 25 / The Tea Council Ltd: tea pickers - back cover and page 29 / Tim Parr, The Pig Improvement Company Ltd: pig breeds - page 10 / Stuart Revell, Genus Freezing Unit, Clwyd: AI picture - page 11 / The Farming Information Centre: sheep dipping - page 12 / The Hutchison Library of Holland Park Ltd: nomadic herdsman - page 13 / National Dairy Council and the Milk Marketing Board - pages 14-15 / Food and Agriculture Organization of the United Nations: statistics for charts - pages 24, 26 and general material for other pages / Fyffes Group Ltd: main picture of banana plantation - pages 28-29 / The Malaysian Rubber Producers' Research Association: latex curing / Tate and Lyle Sugars: sugar cane cutter / The Brazilian Embassy Library: copaiba tree - page 29 / FMG Timberjack Group: tree harvester - pages 30-31 / Renault Agriculture: tractor in orchard - page 32 / Reed Farmers Publishing Group: irrigation devices - page 35 / Zefa Picture Library: vegetables - page 38 / Scottish Salmon Board: fish farming - page 42 / Caroline Penn: food aid trucks / Holt Studios International: mealybugs and wasp / WaterAid: handpump project page 45 / General information provided throughout by: The Royal Agricultural Society of England, The Centre for World Development Education, The Commonwealth Institute, The London Food Commission, The Ministry of Fisheries and Food (Publications Division), The National Farmers' Union, OXFAM, Save the Children Fund, The World Health Organization, War On Want.

Index

Agribusiness, 21, 36, 46
alligators, 43
artificial insemination, 11, 46

Bacteria, 7, 12, 20, 21, 27
bananas, 28-29, 45
barley, 9, 20, 21, 24
beans, 9, 20, 21, 24, 27, 38
bees, 20
biogas, 21, 46
boars, wild, 16
breeding, 11, 12, 37, 43, 46
  crossbreeding, 11, 19, 46
  selective, 9, 11, 31, 32, 36, 45, 47
breeds, 11, 39, 46
buffaloes, 4, 14, 26
bulls, 11

Camels, 4
cash crops, 28, 46
cassava, 6, 22, 24, 45
cattle, 10, 12, 13, 39, 43
  beef, 10, 14, 33
  dairy, 6, 10, 14-15
cereals, 6, 9, 16, 20, 21, 24-25, 46
chemicals, 3, 12, 6, 7, 8, 13, 21, 36, 37, 38, 39, 45
chickens, 18, 23, 38
chlorophyll, 8
climates, 3, 6, 25, 26, 33, 43
coffee, 6, 28
compost, 38, 39
conservation (of land), 40-41
cotton, 6, 28, 35
cows, 11, 14-15, 42
crocodiles, 43
crop rotation, 21, 38, 46
cultivation, 3, 9, 22, 23, 25, 26, 46, 47

Dairy products, 14, 44
DDT, 37
deer, 14, 42, 43
desertification, 7, 40, 46
deserts, 4, 6, 7, 12, 13, 34, 40
diseases, 31, 45
  of livestock, 13, 15
  of people, 27, 44, 45
  of plants, 37, 45
ducks, 18, 19, 20

Eggs, 10, 18, 19, 20, 26, 37, 42, 43
elephants, 30
energy, 4, 8, 18, 24, 33, 36, 38
environments, controlled, 32
erosion (of soil), 7, 23, 30, 40-41, 44, 47

Famines, 40, 45
farming,
  arable, 36
  battery, 18, 19, 46
  dairy, 14 -15
  extensive, 12, 46
  factory, 3, 17, 46
  fish, 42
  free-range, 18
  intensive, 13, 17, 21, 25, 32, 36-37, 38, 46
  livestock, 10-11, 13, 36, 42-43
  mixed, 20-21, 23
  organic, 38-39, 46
  pig, 16-17
  poultry, 3, 18-19
  slash and burn, 22-23, 40, 47
  traditional, 22, 38
fertilizers, 3, 10, 12, 13, 20, 21, 22, 23, 25, 26, 27, 32, 35, 36, 37, 38, 39, 45, 46

firewood, 4, 21, 23, 40
fish, 23, 26, 27, 42
fishing, 22
flowers, 31, 32
food aid, 45
food chains, 37
food mountains, 36, 44, 46
forestry, 30-31, 45, 46
forests, 16, 22, 23, 30, 31
  destruction of, 22, 23, 30, 40
fruit, 6, 9, 20, 22, 23, 28, 32, 36, 38
fuels, 10, 21, 23, 29, 30, 44

Game, 43
geese, 18, 19
genetic engineering, 36, 46
goats, 8, 10, 12, 13, 14
grains, 6, 8, 9, 24, 25, 26, 27, 36, 44
grapes, 32
grasses, 3, 7, 12, 20, 24, 33, 40, 41
grasslands, 6, 12, 13
grazing, 7, 12-13, 27, 40

Harvesters, 32
  combine, 4, 25, 27
  steam-powered, 4
  tree, 31
harvesting, 25, 27, 28, 42, 46
hens, 18, 19
herds, 4, 12, 14
honey, 20, 23
horses, 4
horticulture, 32-33, 46
humus, 6, 7, 22, 23, 46
hunter-gatherers, 4
hunting, 4, 22, 43
husbandry, animal, 3, 10, 39, 46
hydroponics, 33, 46

Insects, 7, 18, 36, 37, 38, 39, 45
irrigation, 32, 33, 34-35, 45, 46

Livestock, 6, 10-11, 12, 20, 21, 24, 36, 38, 39, 42, 44, 46
llamas, 6, 10

Machines,
  diesel-powered, 4
  high-technology, 3, 13, 21, 36
  milking, 14-15
maize, 9, 24, 39
meat, 10, 11, 13, 14, 16, 18, 20, 24, 26, 36, 42, 43, 44
milk, 10, 11, 13, 14, 15, 20, 44, 46
milking, 14-15
millet, 24
minerals, 6, 8, 9, 19, 35
monocultures, 28, 46
monsoons, 26, 27, 46

Nitrates, 6, 8, 27, 46
nutrients, 6, 7, 21, 22, 33, 38, 47

Oats, 20, 24
orchards, 16, 20, 28, 32
ostriches, 42
overgrazing, 40, 45
oxen, 4

Paddy fields, 26-27, 46
peas, 9, 20, 21, 24, 27, 38
pest control, 39
pesticides, 36, 37, 39, 45, 46
pests, 13, 36, 37, 45
photosynthesis, 8, 47

pigs, 11, 16-17, 20, 23, 38, 42
plantains, 22, 28
plantations, 28-29, 30, 31, 38, 40, 47
plants, 6, 7, 8, 9, 22, 27, 32, 33, 37, 38, 40
ploughs, 4, 10, 26
pollination, 31
pollution, 37
ponds, 23, 42
population growth, 44
potatoes, 8, 9, 20, 21, 22
pumps, 26, 34, 35, 45

Ranches, 12, 43
rice, 6, 9, 24, 26-27. 27
roots, 6, 8, 9, 20, 21, 24, 27, 28, 33, 40
rubber, 6, 23, 28, 29, 38
rye, 24

Salt pans, 35, 47
seeds, 8, 9, 22, 23, 24, 26, 28, 30, 40, 41, 45
selective breeding, 9, 11, 31, 32, 36, 45, 47
sheep, 3, 8, 10, 12, 13, 14, 21, 42, 43
silage, 13, 20, 39, 47
silk moths, 43
soil, 3, 6, 7, 8, 21, 22, 23, 26, 27, 33, 35, 38, 39, 40-41
soil erosion, 7, 23, 30, 40 41, 44, 47
sorghum, 24
sugar, 9, 28, 29

Tea, 28, 29
terraces, 27, 40, 41, 47
threshing, 25, 27, 47
tools, 4, 26, 45
tractors, 4, 28, 37
trees, 7, 22, 23, 28, 29, 40
turkeys, 18, 19

Vegetables, 6, 9, 21, 23, 26, 32, 38, 39, 44
vineyards, 28, 32
vitamins, 9, 16, 26

Warthogs, African, 16
waterwheels, 4, 5
wells, 34, 45
wheat, 9, 20, 21, 24, 32, 36
windmills, 4
winnowing, 25, 27, 47
woodland, 6, 20
worms, 6, 7, 13, 37, 39

Yaks, 6, 14
yogurt, 14, 15

Zebu, 14

First published in 1994 by Usborne Publishing Ltd, 83-85 Saffron Hill, London EC1N 8RT, England. Copyright © 1994 Usborne Publishing Ltd.

The name Usborne and the device ♥ are Trade Marks of Usborne Publishing Ltd. All rights reserved. No part of this publication may be reproduced, stored in a retrieval system or transmitted in any form or by any means, electronic, mechanical, photocopying, recording or otherwise, without the prior permission of the publisher.

Printed in Spain